John Hawk

A Seminole Saga

Coacoochee, (Wild Cat)

Coacoochee

John Hawk

A Seminole Saga

Beatrice Levin

Roberts Rinehart Publishers

IN COOPERATION WITH
THE COUNCIL FOR INDIAN EDUCATION

ISBN 1-57098-000-4

Library of Congress Catalog Number 94-066098

Cover art courtesy of the Florida State Archives

Published in the United States by
Roberts Rinehart Publishers
Post Office Box 666
Niwot, Colorado 80544

Distributed in the
U.S. and Canada by
Publishers Group West

Published in Ireland by
Roberts Rinehart
Trinity House, Charleston Road
Ranelaigh, Dublin 6

The Council for
Indian Education Series

THE COUNCIL FOR INDIAN EDUCATION is a non-profit organization devoted to teacher training and to the publication of materials to aid in Indian education. All books are selected by an Indian editorial board and are approved for use with Indian children. Proceeds are used for the publication of more books for Indian children. Roberts Rinehart Publishers copublishes select manuscripts to aid the Council for Indian Education in the distribution of these books to wider markets, to aid in the production of books, and to support the Council's educational programs.

Preface

John Hawk: A Seminole Saga is the story of a runaway son of
a master and a slave who becomes a chief of the Seminole
Indians.

The Seminole wars fell between two American conflicts
that captured the imagination of the American public: the
Mexican-American War and the Civil War. Few novels re-
count the horror and the hostilities of the Seminole wars.

One participant, Ethan Allen Hitchcock, later a United
States general, wrote his brother in 1840: "Five years ago I
came as a volunteer, willingly making every effort in my power
to be of service in punishing, as I thought, the Indians. I now
come with the persuasion that the Indians have been
wronged. I enter upon one of the most hopeless tasks that was
ever given to man to perform."

After the Red Stick War, the Creek Indians migrated to
what was Spanish Florida. Legends abound about the Creek
mother who, during a hail of rifle bullets at Horseshoe Bend,
pretended to be dead. She threw her body over her infant son
to save his life. That baby would grow up to be Osceola, one
of the best-known of American Indian heroes. Later, the
mother walked to Florida, where the Seminoles settled and
provided sanctuary to black runaways. Slave owners came to
hate the Seminoles, who lived independently in wild orange
country. The Seminole villages became the target of land-
hungry Georgians and Alabamans.

In 1817 the Seminoles demanded that the United States government leave them alone. In a military expedition unauthorized by Washington, Gen. Andrew Jackson invaded Seminole country in Spanish Florida. Jackson claimed there had been border incidents involving Seminole Indians and white Georgians. War between the army and the Seminoles lasted off and on for the next four decades.

The United States bought Florida from Spain in 1819. With Spain out of Florida, the last European left the Southeast.

The Seminole wars never really ended, for the Indians never signed a treaty with the United States to recognize the end of hostilities.

1

When the boy saw that he had caught a rabbit in the trap he had set, a whoop of joy came from his throat. It was his thirteenth birthday, and his father had sent him to visit his mother on another plantation. He had left his cabin that morning with his father's ax and a sharp pocketknife that his father had given him as a present. He carried an old book of Bible stories and his battered hat full of ripe peaches.

As John gathered twigs and dried wood for a fire to roast his rabbit, he thought about how delighted his mother had been while he read to her the story of Joseph and his brothers. No other slave on either his master-father's or his slave-mother's plantation could read. Reading had come easily and naturally to John, and nothing gave him more pleasure than a good book. When he had read his mother the story, he saw pride in her misty eyes. His mother had hugged him over and over, covering his face with kisses. Then she had whispered that he must not brag about reading. It was against the law to teach slaves to read. He would remember her warning.

John had many privileges on his father's plantation, but he could not forget that he was a slave until his father freed him. Even then, he might be kidnapped and sold back into slavery.

He felt sad as he rubbed two sticks together to get a spark for his fire. Soon a little blaze picked up like a tiny red flag licking at the twigs. Hungry, eager, he waited for the wood to burn and the smoke to disappear like wispy ghosts in the forest. With his birthday knife, he skinned and cleaned the rabbit, and set the hide to dry in the sun. Satisfied that the pocketknife was very sharp, he cleaned it carefully on the bark of a sassafras tree.

When the fire became glowing coals, John made a fork of a green stick and skewered the rabbit liver to toast it. The flames of fire were like tongues of red gold. He ate the liver in one piping hot mouthful. It was delicious. John had had nothing to eat since the chitlings in his mother's cabin long hours earlier. What a good birthday it had been, seeing his half brothers and sisters, his cousins, none of whom even knew what day *they* were born, let alone how old they were. John felt a moment of pride — "braggin'," his mother would have said — that his father had kept birth records for him and observed his birthday every year. Thirteen years old. Born July 1, 1801.

Sticking two forked branches into the ground on either side of the fire, John skewered the rabbit on a third branch and strung it between them, creating a handy spit on which to roast his meat. A breeze lifted the leaves of the trees and blew a few sparks from the fire. John quickly stamped them out. He turned the rabbit on the spit, its juices spattering into the red-hot fire. The embers turned to ash. It seemed to John that a secret city lay in the fire, like the cities he had never seen: cities of the Bible, or of Old England or of New England of his father's storytelling. Somewhere people heard music, laughed at pageants and puppets, went to plays, and walked on streets lined with shops. What a different world that would be, like the one in the embers of the fire — so strange, almost beyond imagining to a slave living all his life on a Georgia plantation.

He longed to see a city. He longed to see the sea. John lay back, gazing up at the blue sky through the dark leaves of the trees. The heat of the day was heavier than the heat from his fire.

"That rabbit do smell good," said a soft voice behind him.

Startled, John sat up, grabbing his father's ax, ready to defend himself. The slaves knew that there was always danger of being kidnapped and sold miles from familiar faces and their own plantations.

"Who're you?" John demanded, holding the ax by its handle.

"Hey, don't get jumpy," the fellow said. Short, slight, red-skinned, naked to the waist, broad-shouldered, bow and arrow in his small hands, this visitor had to be an Indian, John thought. John's father had told him stories about Indians scalping people and inflicting other cruel tortures. A cold shiver ran up his spine as he stared at the dark, restless eyes and the long, black hair hanging over the Indian's forehead. The young man had a straight pointed nose, chiseled lips, and a friendly expression. He replied, "Osceola's my name."

"What kind of name is that?"

"Seminole," Osceola replied, lifting the spit on which the rabbit was roasting. "It's cooked. Let's eat!"

John laughed good-naturedly and put aside his father's ax. "There's enough for two," he agreed. With his sharp knife, he cut the rabbit into pieces and set them on a clean stone between them. "My name's John White," he said. "Have a peach!" They each picked a ripe peach from John's battered old hat. Osceola bit into the fresh fruit. The sweet juice ran down his chin. He brushed away the liquid with a sweep of his red-brown hand and grinned a big grin. He sure did not look like a fierce scalping Indian to John. "It's my birthday," John said. "I'm thirteen. How old are you?"

Osceola looked into the distance. "I already fought in a war."

"Not braggin'—a'course," John grinned. That was what his mother always said to him when he offered her a brag or two.

"I did! I fought the United States Army!"

John could hardly hide his amazement. For a moment there, he had been proud he could celebrate a birthday and this new acquaintance could not. But a boy his own age who had fought in a war!

Osceola said, "I'm a brave."

"I'm brave too," John responded hotly.

"I'm a warrior," Osceola insisted.

"Tell me . . ." John loved stories.

Osceola had the Indian love of storytelling, and he liked an audience. He pointed at John and began his story, telling John that in Georgia his tribe was called Red Sticks. The Red Sticks protected runaway slaves. But a rival tribe, the Creeks from Alabama, wanted to have slaves. The Creeks joined with the United States Army to fight the Red Sticks.

John leaned forward. "Tell me more," he begged.

Osceola told how his mother woke him up one night when a big yellow moon shone almost as bright as a sun. "My mother shook me, 'Boy, get up, hurry, many, many white warriors come.'" She pushed his bow and arrow at him and ran with the women and children to hide in the high corn stalks.

Osceola, from behind a tree, saw the militia and the Creeks attacking. The Red Sticks had great courage, but they had only bows and arrows that they shot from the cornfield. The soldiers had muskets. Their bullets flew and hit many Red Sticks, who finally had to flee to the forests, still sending their arrows toward their enemies. At Horseshoe Bend, soldiers killed over a thousand of the Red Stick braves.

Osceola fell silent, for a moment carried away by his own story. John could hardly believe that a boy his own age could have shot arrows at United States soldiers. Osceola, pleased that he had impressed his new friend, continued, telling how the Red Stick survivors, among them his grandmother, his mother, and many children, walked from the Tallapoosa River to the Yellow Water River.

Osceola helped himself to another piece of roasted rabbit. His voice, John thought, was higher and shriller than those of slaves on the plantation. He talked like a white man.

"I like to chew the rabbit bones," Osceola said. John admired the Indian's tea-colored skin, almost the color of the dark copper kettle hanging in the fireplace of his father's house.

Osceola said, "You ain't got real black skin."

"My father is white."

"You got stiff hair." He ran his hand playfully over the tightly curled black hair. John pushed Osceola's hand away.

"Where you from?" John wanted to know.

"I was born near the Tallapoosa River—my mother told me." Osceola wiped his hands on some grass and said, "That there was one good rabbit!"

"Where did you learn English?"

"First from Powell, my Scottish stepfather, and from Peter McQueen, my mother's uncle. And from runaway blacks . . . That's where we get our name 'Seminole'—it means runaways. Want to hear me speak Indian tongue?"

John nodded, curious. He was amazed, attentive, full of wonder as Osceola began to make sounds that seemed to mimic the singing of birds, a prattling like that of infants. It was a lovely language—gentle, musical. John thought Osceola never made the sound of an R. But as the Indian spoke he moved his hands and his head as if to emphasize each word. His eyebrows climbed up and down his forehead. Speaking, he seemed more man than boy. He became dignified and placid, his features heroic and brave. Yes, John could believe that Osceola had been in battle, that he was a brave, a warrior. He felt a moment of awe.

Osceola must have had an inkling of this awe, for he stopped and said, "We got black men in Cuscowilla. Some live in their own villages near ours. They's free."

"Free!" The word struck John's heart like the ringing of the Liberty Bell. Free!

"Acourse," Osceola continued. "Blacks own horses, cows, and pigs. No Indian takes them animals from the blacks."

John's heart began to beat fast. "They's free?" he questioned softly, hardly above a whisper. He did not feel so brave now.

"They's free!" Osceola repeated. "They build houses, they farm, hunt, fish. They dress like Seminoles. Blacks carry guns. . ."

John held his breath, wondering if he should believe everything Osceola told him.

"Where you from?" Osceola asked.

"Near here. My father's plantation."

"You a slave?"

John made no move to reply. He was as afraid to lie as he was to confess.

"Trust me," Osceola assured him. "Ain't we friends?"

John had had few lessons in trust. He shook his head, afraid to believe what Osceola told him. Osceola offered his hand. In truth, even Osceola had little reason to trust the world, for his father was a shadowy figure who had disappeared from his life. And he had early learned caution. As a little boy, he would approach his own village after hunting, carefully flattening himself behind a tree to make sure everything was normal. And had he not walked with his ragged family for months, hungry, eating only roots, berries, and fish?

John had seen his father shake hands over business deals, in the sale of peaches, pigs, or slaves. He shook hands with Osceola. John felt mature, having shaken hands for the first time in his life. He liked the man-to-man feeling he had with this newfound friend.

"I been to see my mother on her plantation. I get to see her on my birthday and sometimes at Christmas."

"How come you ain't livin' with her?" Osceola demanded.

"My father sold her. He didn't want to. His wife made him. She's a white witch. She'd beat me day and night if my father didn't stop her."

"Your mother—she's a slave?" Osceola picked up a stick and began to draw in the sand.

John nodded.

"With our people, a man belongs to his mother's clan. My mother's Muskogee, so I'm Muskogee. An Indian stays with his mother's clan. Why don't you live with your mother?"

John didn't want to tell Osceola that he had no choice; he lived where the white man told him to. He wasn't yet a full "taskable," a field worker. He could sometimes join white and black children playing noisily and mischievously together. On soft summer evenings, after sundown, an old slave might tell folk tales of his African childhood, stories all the children loved. There was always a slave who could translate Ibo or Ashanti into English so that everyone could enjoy the stories.

The slaves had their own little gardens, pigs, and chickens. Sometimes in the dusk the children enjoyed a treat of baked yams or chicken. These slaves were John's "family." He knew and loved them.

"Run away," Osceola urged. "Indians and blacks live free in Florida. Our clan's walking there. Come with me."

John thought it was easy for Osceola to urge him to run off. The Indian wasn't risking being beaten half to death. Cold fear touched John. Run away! The idea struck terror to his heart. Run away! Leave the plantation forever. Never again see his mother or father? Would he dare?

He scrambled to the creek, shucked his pants, and jumped in, naked. The water parted noisily with his body. He splashed and howled in the sharp cold. The creek, fed from underground springs, was always frigid, even in the heat of southern summers.

"Come on in, Osceola!" John challenged.

It was the first time John spoke the name of the boy who would be his companion in great adventure, his lifelong friend. Osceola, laughing, pulled off his leggings and moccasins and metal ornaments and plunged into the rushing water. The creek, running swiftly over large smooth rocks and sandy bottom, was clear and clean as dawn.

"*Yasi-ola!*" yelled the Indian boy, his voice rising in a spine-tingling, ear-piercing shriek. "Cold!" He grabbed John's head and ducked it under water. They wrestled, testing each other's strength, their feet shuffling on the slippery bottom of the creek where mud and stones gave them no footing. They were well-matched. John was taller, but the Indian was more muscular and stronger. Neither could best the other. Breathless, they gazed into each other's black eyes and affirmed their friendship. They dog-paddled along by the grassy knoll, now and then grinning at each other. Friends.

Naked, dripping wet, they came out of the water and lay on the grass. The sun felt good as the cool pearls of water dried on the skin. They ate the rest of the peaches from John's hat.

"I like fuzzy peach skin," Osceola said. He opened the peach pit and removed the seed. After digging a little hole with a stick, he planted the seed.

Sometimes the slaves came to this clear creek for a day of picnicking and swimming. John knew the area well.

Would I run away? The question boggled his mind. Running away was not a new idea. He had long considered it. A boy or man could not be a slave and not think of running away.

"My people are going to Cuscowilla. The Spanish will leave us alone there. Walk with me." Osceola shook an accusing finger at John. "You! John. You gonna be a slave all your life?"

The idea was cruel. Often on waking in the mornings, John would think of his father's big white house, the carpets, paintings, the fancy furniture. The kitchen slaves ate wheat cakes and drank coffee with cream. His father had bacon and a big breakfast. John would gaze around at the dark, unpainted splintery boards of the cabin, at the stiff, smelly straw sacks on which he and the other slave boys slept. He would get up before dawn and dress in the same old dirty rags. His breakfast was corn mush without milk or butter on it. He went barefoot all day, picking peaches and corn, or tending the hogs. He longed for something better. Now and then, he could get a book from his father's house, and he would hide in the woods until dark to read after a supper of chitterlings.

"I might never see my mother again," John said. "I would maybe miss my father. He ain't mean."

"He sold your mother!" Osceola said angrily.

"He learned me to read the Bible. I know the story of Joseph and his brothers."

"Great balls of fire!" Osceola bounced a stone across the surface of the rushing creek. "Go back to the plantation," he said in disgust. "Anyone who thinks a slave is a hero ain't no brave."

Osceola's scorn hurt.

"Joseph was a slave in Egypt. He got to be a hero," John said in a slow, thoughtful way. He told Osceola the story of how Joseph saved his brothers, even after they had sold him into slavery.

"You go back to that there plantation," Osceola insisted, "you ain't no brave."

John longed to be a brave. The core of resistance to the idea of running away was shrinking. He wanted to be convinced.

"You gonna be free!" Osceola shoved him and he fell over backwards. Before John could recover, Osceola snatched up John's hat and raced away with it, jumping over shrubs and underbrush. John pushed himself to his feet and tried to catch the fleet-footed Indian who leapt over fallen trees as if the way were clear and open.

"Come on! Run away!" shrieked Osceola, and gave a blood-curdling yell, "*Yasi-ollllla!*"

Catching a low thick branch, Osceola stepped up on a fallen limb of a tree and swung like a monkey. At last, breathless, Osceola dropped down and shoved the hat down on John's head. "Come with me!"

His request became a command. Solemnly, John offered Osceola his hand. They shook more seriously than they had the first time. He and Osceola started to pick blackberries growing on a low thorny bush. They filled John's hat. John took up his father's ax, his birthday knife, and his Bible. He and Osceola, with his bow and arrow, began clearing the path through the Georgia forest. Neither of them could know what adventures they would share.

"Maybe you had in mind to take off from that there planta-tion," Osceola challenged. "You got an ax, a knife, and a hat, ain't you? That's travelin' stuff."

For a moment, John felt that Osceola knew him better than he knew himself.

They walked through the forest for hours. Osceola had seen an alligator, which he described to John. Who would believe there was such a creature? That Osceola has got a good imag-ination, John thought. He only hoped that what the Indian said about Cuscowilla was the God's honest truth.

When it was too dark to go on, they lay down and slept be-side each other while the crickets and the hoot owls filled the night with song.

The bright morning sun awoke John. Above him, the dark leaves of the trees shivered and danced in the breeze. He did not know where he was. He could not recall how he had come here. The sight of a doe with serene eyes staring at him in wonder lifted John's heart. How beautiful and calm the doe seemed.

Osceola stretched and sat up. "Oh, we got a ways to walk yet," he told John. He reached for a handful of berries from John's hat. The boys made short work of breakfast.

Osceola looked at John's dirty feet. Blood had dried on his cut toes. His legs were badly scratched. John had used the rabbit skin and his book of Bible stories for a pillow. Osceola borrowed John's knife and cut the rabbit skin in half and then the edges of each half he cut into attached ribbons. These he shaped, fur side inside, around John's feet, tying the long strips up around his ankles. The rabbit's ears Osceola tucked into the heels of the moccasins.

"I bet I make the best fur boots in the world," Osceola declared.

"Not braggin', acourse." John playfully punched his friend's naked chest. He was too grateful for words.

Osceola walked ahead with the animalish walk of a hunter, of a boy who had stalked game all his life. John carried his father's ax, his knife, and his Bible. Osceola wore the old hat John's father had given him. Here and there, where the un-

11

derbrush gave way to a sandy narrow road, the boys could see the prints left by a deer's delicate hooves. Osceola pointed to a heavier print. "Black bear," he said.

A spiritual gaze came into Osceola's eye. John thought he had a beguiling smile of gentleness. "I be proud to share the woods with animals." They walked in silence for a while. "Do you like ball games?" Osceola asked. John shook his head.

"We have a pole on Green Corn Dance. We try to hit it with a deerskin ball stuffed with deer hair," Osceola said. "Girls use their hands to throw the balls, but the boys have to catch or pick up the ball with a pair of rackets." John hoped he would have a chance to try his luck at such a game.

They crossed many meandering streams, stopping to drink and wash at each one. The boys paddled their feet in the clear running water, or plunged in and swam across the narrow rapids. At every opportunity, Osceola wrestled John to the ground. The Indian bested John every time.

"This ain't like Okefenokee," Osceola said. "That there swamp in Georgia, my people named 'land of the trembling earth.'"

John liked the sound . . . land of the trembling earth . . . and repeated it to himself as they walked along. How he would like to see it. "They's alligators there?" He wanted to hear Osceola tell him again.

"Lotsa alligators. And swamp frogs growlin' in the grass. And wadin' birds with them long, skinny legs."

"You swim there?"

"Naw, the water's black—full of cypress sap. You got marsh grass and hurrah bush jungle. And snakes."

John's father had told him about snakes, but he had never seen one. He shivered with apprehension. The land of the trembling earth. What a good name the Indians had picked.

Frightened by the boys, a wild turkey flew into the air, flapping its wings furiously and rising so suddenly that John was as scared as the fowl. Had he reacted faster, he might have killed the turkey with his ax, and the boys could have had a meal.

At midday, while they paddled their feet in a pool, Osceola announced he was hungry. He told John to build a fire. John, wondering what Osceola planned to cook, gathered sticks and twigs and flat stones. Osceola, lying on his stomach with his hands in the water, suddenly let out that yell that John now recognized as his friend's special cry: "*Yasi-ola!*"

Osceola jumped to his feet, a huge turtle in his hands. But John had not yet started the fire, and Osceola demanded with a scowl, "Do I gotta do it all?"

With one swift blow of the ax, the turtle was dead. Osceola rubbed two sticks together until he got a spark, and soon the fire was blazing and the turtle cooking in its shell. Above them, a startled wood duck exploded into flight. The boys quenched their thirst with scooped handfuls of clean water. The turtle shell was the bowl, and they ate every bit of the meat. They rested, listening to the calls of the birds, the cries of gulls, and the rustling leaves. This is what it is like to be free, John thought gratefully.

"You be Seminole-born?"

Osceola hesitated before answering. "My mother tell me I be Muskogee because she be Muskogee. My grandmother be Muskogee because her mother—who married a Scot, an old white man named James McQueen, many moons ago—be Muskogee. My mother said my blood be Muskogee for more moons than there be stars in the summer sky."

John felt a surge of joy. Osceola had white blood as John himself did. Osceola's Scottish descendant was maybe a greatgrandfather, but it gave him more in common with John. Good.

Osceola stopped in a clearing to pick small grass tubers growing near a large flat rock. "This here's deer food," he said. "When I was little, we played tops with them." He chose some sharp twigs which he stuck through the center of the tubers. Then he rubbed his palm across the flat rock to clean off sand and pebbles.

"Look here, watch this spin!" Osceola gave it a fast twirl. The homemade top took off and danced on its point, round and round. He handed a top to John, who made several false starts and then succeeded in making the top spin in a lively twirl.

John enjoyed playing, but Osceola said they had to hurry on. On a narrow dirt road, John saw it first: a tree loaded with wild oranges. He snatched his hat from Osceola's head and both boys picked the small ripe fruit. They filled up on oranges, getting juice all over their hands and faces. Osceola saved the seeds and buried them in several small holes.

Day after day, they walked until dark and slept under the sparkling stars. Osceola, with his bow and arrow, killed squirrels, opossums, raccoons, and other small game. Osceola was so stealthy that sometimes he startled John, moving quietly behind him.

The boys skinned the animals, roasted and ate the meat. Soon they had a fine bundle of hides to cover themselves against the cold night.

After many moons, they came to Tallahassee, where the Spaniards had fortified a hill. Giant magnolia trees and great oaks towered over small homes. The Indian villagers lived in simple cabins similar to the homes of the whites. The Indians had cattle, horses, and hogs. Though the boys were welcomed, Osceola was eager to keep going. They left the next morning.

For lunch that day they ate wild berries and fruit and the cooked rice the Indian women had given them. For another five days, they walked toward the gulf. At last, John smelled the sweet salt air of the sea! When they came to the beach, they saw in the distance against huge white clouds the topsails of ships in a small harbor.

Osceola stripped and ran into the water, dog-paddling out so far that John almost lost sight of him. John envied him: Osceola was so manly, so strong, he knew so much. Osceola had always been free. He could act impulsively, could come and go as he liked. His mother had walked on with the tribe to the south, but

Osceola had chosen to stay behind to visit with his teacher. Because he wanted to. John had never been able to do whatever he wanted to. He had worked from sunup to sundown in the fields. And in the evenings, his father sometimes taught him to read and write. Usually, John was too tired to pay attention, and then his father became angry and impatient.

John waded waist-deep into the sea, waving to Osceola and shouting, "Come back!" Genuinely fearful that his friend might drown, John did not want to be left to cope by himself.

The billowing sails of ships white and lovely danced on the blue water. Osceola swam back, diving in and out of the gently rolling waves. The boys lay on the white sand until they were dry. They brushed the sand off each other.

John said he had never been beaten on the plantation. Osceola said he had been punished by his mother — sometimes harshly, by being scratched with something very sharp.

What Osceola hated was working in the fields. That was "women's work," planting beans, corns, potatoes, pumpkins. Still, he always planted a seed if one came into his hand. That was a natural thing to do, he said. But Indian men hunted or slept in the shade while women and children worked the fields.

John nodded. There were things he would far rather do than work in the fields.

Soon the two friends walked toward the docks, where fishing smacks nudged the wharf and ships rocked on the waves.

Osceola ran forward on the wooden wharf and, leaning against a rail, shouted for the captain.

A black-bearded, heavy-set man turned and waved from a small boat.

"Could we hitch a ride to Tampa?" Osceola shouted. The captain glanced from one boy to the other. John held his breath and forced his face into a toothy smile.

The captain glared menacingly from under thick brows. He took off his battered, soiled cap, and scratched his thickly curled hair. John noted the captain's hair was like his own black, wiry, thick. "*Sí*," he said, "*sí sí*."

"You be Cuban?" Osceola asked. John was impressed. That Osceola knows everything! John thought reluctantly, I know nothing.

"Cuban, *sí*. I got no crew. You guys jump een!"

Clutching his father's ax, his knife, his book, and the bundle of animal skins, John felt a strange hot rush of blood flow to his face. Events were moving him into something beyond his control. Once on that boat, there would be no going back ever. He took a running jump and hit the deck of the fishing smack.

"I show you to handle the ropes," the Cuban captain said.

The boys listened while the captain showed them how to raise and lower the sails.

"Good timing," the captain said. "I leave right now."

At the request of the captain, a passing black man gave the boat a huge shove. The boat drifted from the wharf. Following the captain's instructions, John helped raise the sails. The wind picked up and billowed out the great sheets of white sail, and in the brisk breeze, the boat glided smoothly into the open, choppy sea.

This was fun for John. In the twilight, one star gleamed, and he felt the clean wind in his face. He followed the captain below, where, in the galley, the dark man pushed his battered cap to the back of his head and picked up a huge knife.

John, terrorized, fell back against the galley wall and held out both hands as if to ward off a blow. He had seen a slave stabbed to death. But the captain was only about to peel an onion, not someone's Adam's apple. He lay the onion on a board to slice and dice it with quick, skilled strokes.

"Feesh," the captain said to John, who had begun to breathe again, "fresh feesh. The best deesh . . ."

Into a skillet on the stove, the captain poured a little oil, threw in the diced onion, followed by chopped green pepper. The boned fish went into the skillet next. Then he scooped cooked rice into bowls. The captain poured a little wine into the skillet, stirred a few minutes, and then added the fish to the bowls. He handed the bowls to John, indicating they should be set on the galley table.

The night breezes were cool. White sails whipped in the welcome wind above the little fishing smack. The boat smelled of fish, but John found it a pleasant odor. The boys ate with great relish. The captain broke a long, thin loaf of bread into chunks, and with a piece of bread mopped up the last of the sauce and thrust it into his mouth.

The captain said, "Lend me your ax. I got a coconut here."

John had never seen a coconut. He handed his ax to the captain, who split the shell with one blow. The brown head lay open, and sweet fresh coconut milk was poured into a glass and was shared. The captain chopped off chunks of coconut meat with the knifelike edge of the ax.

Now, in the dark sky, the stars twinkled brilliantly like the candles seen through the windows of the plantation house. John thought of the hot cabin that was his home, of the familiar smells of straw, sweat, moldy food, dirty clothes, urine. He would never see that cabin again.

3

Late into the night, the captain told the boys to get some sleep. He could manage by himself

John, comforted by his closeness to Osceola, watched the stars twinkling and whirling in the sky. The boat bobbed beneath him, rocking him to gentle sleep.

When the boys awoke, refreshed, the captain gave them oranges and rice for breakfast. During the day, they took turns throwing fishing nets into the water and bringing up the catch. John, helping with the sails, found his hands raw from holding the ropes.

The captain would stop at Negro Fort to exchange his fish for corn and meat. "Maroons there raise vegetables and cattle."

"Maroons? What's them?"

"Don't you know nothin', son? You be a Maroon. Any run-away black is a free black around here. A Maroon. You gonna settle in Negro Fort with Indians? You be free."

Osceola had heard rumors of Indians who had lost their homes in the Battle of Horseshoe Bend now living in Negro Fort. As the skiff sailed into shore, he saw some Seminoles he thought he recognized. Sure enough, a boy on shore rushed to help pull the skiff up the beach, crying, "It's Osceola!"

Osceola jumped out, and the two boys laughed in excitement at the surprising reunion.

"Is my mother here?" Osceola asked.

"She gone to Cuscowilla near Tampa," he replied.

That night, the Indians and Maroons offered the captain and the boys a feast of a calf roasted on a spit, coontie, and delicious cooked vegetables.

In the morning, they loaded the skiff with corn. Osceola and John left Negro Fort reluctantly. All day and into the evening, the boys helped with the sails. John's back hurt from the unusual strain.

On the third day, the captain sailed the smack gracefully as a seagull into Tampa Bay. Both boys, now familiar with sails and ropes, competently helped the captain. Darkskinned, Spanish-speaking traders shouted to each other and rushed about, offering bundles of furs and hides, baskets of shells, fish, oysters, crab.

The captain waved away John's appreciation. "You help me," he insisted, "I help you." He gave them each a bunch of bananas and some Spanish coins.

John pulled his father's hat low over his face — not that he expected to be recognized so far from the plantation. But a runaway slave was valuable to anyone, either to be returned to a master or to be sold to another master.

Osceola asked around on the deck for anyone who spoke English. Finally, a woman in a long dress and a bonnet replied in accented English. Osceola wanted directions to Cuscowilla. She said she was the wife of a missionary, and she had recently been to Cuscowilla. On a piece of paper, she drew a rough map to guide them.

As they walked through Tampa, Osceola talked about his mother. "Her people be Red Sticks — brave, good people. The other Creeks — White Sticks — cowards. They fight on the side of the whites."

"White Sticks be enemies of Red Sticks?" John was amazed. Would Indians fight each other?

"John, learn this: to interrupt someone is bad manners."

At the plantation, the slaves all talked at once. John

hushed. He would learn that all Seminoles considered inter-
ruption rude.

Following the map, they found themselves in a forest at
noon. John chopped through thick underbrush with his ax,
while Osceola used John's knife to cut away the thorny bushes.
Sawgrass tore cruelly at their legs through the ragged pants.
The swamp steamed in the sun, baking brutally on open un-
shaded areas.

Osceola knelt to pick up some white feathers. "An egret
lost these." He put them in his black hair, tightening and fas-
tening them with a twig. "My fetish!" he declared.

John, envious, wished he had a fetish too. Whatever a
fetish was, he wanted one. He wasn't going to be a monkey, for
sure. He wasn't going to stick feathers in his hair. He knocked
off some bark from a sassafras tree with his ax. Handing a piece
to Osceola, he chewed on a piece as they struggled through
dense tropical forest. Did Osceola know they were walking in
the right direction?

"When our people escaped Georgia, I got good at gettin'
turkey with my bow and arrow."

"Not braggin', acourse," John muttered.

"We had a hundred people to feed, old people like my
Grandmother Ann . . ."

John's heart lifted when they came at last to a real road and
Osceola pointed to the first sign of Indian life. A Seminole family—mother, father, two children—were trotting along at a
brisk pace on beautiful horses. Behind the horses, pack animals
followed, heavily laden with game, hides, and a dead deer, the
arrow still in it. Osceola raced like a swift animal to catch up
with them, shouting until the father stopped and turned.

"Be this the way to Cuscowilla?" Osceola demanded.

"It be," the father assured him. He offered him a fawnskin
of honey.

John held up a hand in protest. "No, thanks."

Osceola gave John a withering glance as he accepted the

fawnskin with appreciation. Osceola muttered to John, "Never refuse the offer of a gift."

John thought the Indian girl was beautiful. The mother, her long braids almost to her waist, dismounted the horse. She removed the hides from one mule to the other and told the two boys to mount the bareback mule.

Half asleep with exhaustion, John sat up behind Osceola, resting his head on his friend's shoulder. They'd had little sleep on the boat and had walked a long way through pine and palmetto thickets and under a hot sun. Now the caravan moved steadily on the dusty road, and John seemed to dream. He wet his lips with his tongue. His hand rested on the fawnskin of honey. The thought of honey made him even more thirsty.

By nightfall, tired and hungry, John almost wished himself back in the filthy cabin on his father's plantation. There would be chitlings, sweet potatoes and peelings from carrots, and bits of vegetables cooking in a stew. His mouth was dry and his every muscle ached. Now in dense darkness, he heard sounds of drumming, voices of children, and the earth seemed young again.

They had come at last to Cuscowilla. The Indian woman slid off her horse. Moving like a spirited shadow, she lifted her son from his horse and placed him, still asleep, on the wood planks of their little palmetto house.

Jumping from the mule, Osceola ran toward a woman whose open arms invited an embrace. With a dignified gesture, as she stood in the light of a glowing fire, she took both her son's hands. Holding him at arm's length, she said, "You are returned."

The strong resemblance between mother and son touched John. Would he ever again see his own mother? John's father had told him that Indians did not show emotion. Yet John thought Osceola's mother was greeting her Indian son with the same emotional intensity that his own mother showed whenever he had arrived at the Stone Plantation. The affection between mother and son was as obvious as the resemblance.

"This be my friend, John," Osceola said to his mother.

"You must be hungry," Osceola's mother said. "Come eat."

Osceola's mother wore a calico tunic and leggings on which she had hung strings of deer hooves that made a rhythmic sound when she walked. Now, all three squatted around the fire. The juices of a wild turkey on a spit dripped into the red embers. Osceola's mother rolled coontie corn flour in her hands, wrapped the flour in a cabbage of the palmetto tree, and lay the rolls to bake. With a sharp small knife, she cut off pieces of wild turkey roasting on a spit and offered each boy a piece. The turkey was deliciously tender. The boys drank the hot tea the mother had brewed from the sassafras bark of the swamps.

Osceola's mother spoke in low murmuring tones to her son.

Osceola told John, "She worried about how long it took for us to get here. She say there be cougars 'round the hammock, much game, much wild turkeys. The women planted corn, cabbage, sweet potatoes. We have enough food. She say you be welcome, but maybe be safer at Negro Fort. No slave catchers go there."

John shuddered with fear when two huge, shadowy figures with knives in their hands appeared before him in the fire-light. But they were only Indians about to cut off a chunk of roast turkey.

John had liked the people at Negro Fort and several girls had urged him to remain there. But John was reluctant to be separated from Osceola.

"We can go back there any time," Osceola told John. His mother did not object. In the firelight, John saw a sadness come into her eyes. She offered him the hot baked cabbage rolls, and he ate until he was satisfied.

Suddenly, a blood-curdling cry rent the air. "Yo-ho-heeeeeeee!!!"

John jumped to his feet, dropping the turkey wing on which he had chewed. "God almighty, what's that?"

"The Seminole cry of danger!"

"Cougar!" yelled someone. The warriors poured out of log and palmetto huts with bows and arrows, racing toward the cries. A young girl, darker than John, her blue eyes reflecting the light of the fire, came close to ask John if he wanted to chase the cougar. John felt too tired to be a hero.

"I be a runaway slave too," she said.

"Then you go with us to this place, Negro Fort?" John wondered.

"No. This be my village now. I married a Seminole. Children of such marriages be free."

In the distance, a high cry of triumph indicated the cougar had been killed. Soon the Indians dragged the huge bloodied cat to the fire. Children gathered to stroke the soft fur and wonder at the large head.

The young girl squatted on the ground beside John and spoke of the kindness she had known since living among the Indians. "They be the first people who ever treated me like a human being," she said. "What do you call yourself?"

"John White." He saw her strange look. A black called white.

"What be your name?" John asked.

"My name was Hortense when I was a slave. Everyone called me Horrible Hortense. Horry for short. But when I come here, I changed my name to Evening Star."

What a pretty name, John thought.

"My people call me Star," she said, "but the slaves who know me when I come call me Horry."

That night, sleeping on a straw mat next to Osceola, John considered assuming an Indian name. In the morning, he asked Osceola, "What do your name mean?"

"Rising Sun."

"I would like a name meaning something," John said. What about Rising Moon? John Moon, John Sun? No, he would not like a name that sounded like Johnson, a man who had been a cruel overseer on the plantation. Against the clean and clear morning sky, a hawk rose and soared. "Hawk!" exclaimed John aloud. "I be John Hawk and I fly free!"

Osceola agreed. "John Hawk. A good name."

John stirred, and through the open door of the palmetto cabin, he surveyed the flight of the hawk, swooping, soaring. The sudden appearance of the hawk seemed an omen of good times to come. John Hawk — a new name, a new life. John Hawk would be happy and, best of all, free. Free!

4

John Hawk lived two years at Cuscowilla, hunting and fishing. Sometimes he worked with the women in the fields. Few Seminole men ever helped with the planting, but John Hawk felt pride in teaching the women what he had learned on the plantation. And they taught him Indian ways.

John thought the Seminole women beautiful. He watched a young girl wash her hair in a lather made of saponine roots. It was the same concoction that Osceola's mother had given John for his morning bath in the creek. The slim girl's skin shone like polished copper. Her hair seemed to him like raven's wings. He admired the sound of the women's voices, like bird song, like the rustling of leaves in the trees.

Hunting in the woods with Osceola one day, John had just bagged a doe when Osceola gave a whispered warning: "John! A white man!"

Cautiously, the boys crawled under thick shrubs and lay as still as death for a long time. When the danger seemed past, Osceola said, "Lately there be talk of slave catchers around here. Maybe you better move to Negro Fort."

John trembled. Slave catchers! No runaway slave is ever safe. For several weeks, John Hawk refused to consider leaving Cuscowilla. He had not run away from the plantation to hide behind the walls of a fort. But when one of the runaways did not return from fishing, no one assumed he had drowned. Everyone agreed that he must have been kidnapped. Reluctantly, and after much agonizing, John Hawk decided he would be safer at Negro Fort, which was also called Blount's Fort. Osceola would lead John Hawk.

Osceola's mother prepared a deerskin full of food, scraped carrots, coontie flour bread, honey, roast turkey.

All day, Osceola and John walked toward Blount's Fort, stopping only to drink and wash themselves at clear running streams.

"I would like to be free like you," John Hawk muttered.

"I ain't so free." Osceola remembered how the army had razed his village, and how the survivors had walked to Florida, hungry and miserable. The army could attack at any time or force the Indians to move again.

"Tell me about the fort," John urged.

Osceola knew that the British had built this strong fort at Prospect Bluff up the river from the Apalachicola in Spanish Territory. The British, Osceola told John, as they chopped their way through thick jungle, manned the fort with Red Sticks and runaway slaves. When the British left Florida, the runaway blacks remained with a large supply of arms and armaments. Some of the Indians took off, but runaways felt safe there. Renamed Negro Fort, it became a haven for slaves.

After two days of walking in the hot July sun, John spotted at last the rough roof of the fort in the distance. A welcome sight.

Within a week, John Hawk was glad he had come and felt content. Within the fort, women wore Seminole clothes. People lived in homes built of timbers and shingles lashed to posts and rafters with strips of oak. Big muscular blacks polished and cared for the guns they used for hunting wild game. The women wove baskets out of split oak or reeds, some ornamented with pine needles. One of the old women told John that she had learned the patterns she wove in her basket as a little girl in Africa.

Unlike the Indians, who ate whenever they were hungry, sometimes even getting up at night to cut a chunk of meat off a doe or a turkey roasting over a fire, the runaways ate three meals a day. That was the way their masters had taught them.

When they had been in the fort a few weeks, John and Osceola went out to meet new arrivals. Suddenly, Osceola let out a great cry: "Wild Cat!"

Osceola embraced his friend. When he recognized Wild Cat's sister, Chumpee, Osceola seemed deeply moved. He introduced Wild Cat and Chumpee to John, who thought they looked enough alike to be twins.

Chumpee said, "We are twins," and took John's hand in a friendly clasp. How pretty she is, he thought. How he'd like to impress this girl with flashing dark eyes who teased and flirted with him. He was about the same age as the twins.

Chumpee sat cross-legged next to the fire and helped herself to roast deer. John ate in silence, suddenly shy. Chumpee took pity on him and offered, "You know King Philip? He's my father."

John did not know King Philip, but he knew that kings were royalty. Perhaps this lovely girl was a princess. He could hardly take his eyes off her.

For several days, Osceola went off with Wild Cat to fish. John Hawk and Chumpee helped with the milking. Chumpee teased him, "Milking is women's work."

He had often been told that planting and picking yams was women's work. If he had a gun and knew how to use it, he would go hunting with Osceola.

In the hot July sun, John Hawk lay on the rough earth-palisaded roof of the fort and watched the runaways working, outside in the fields and inside with their trades. Shadows moved mysteriously beneath palmetto trees. A speckled doe ran down in the underbrush to the banks of a flowing stream. An old black woman struggled through the thick forest trying to keep her string of silver fish from catching on the branches. The fish shone with a rainbow of colors. That's our dinner, John thought.

Something went slinking in the tall sawgrass — a fox, a cougar, maybe a cat or a rat. Sometimes the slinking would be a frightened black man, fearful of the reception he may find. John, stretching out on the splintery log, stared down at an animal. A cougar! If only he had a gun! Or even Osceola's bow and arrow. He crawled down from the heavy timbers which fenced the fort. Maybe Chumpee would go fishing with him.

A young girl in a skirt of many colors carried a bundle of kindling. Chumpee followed with a woven basket full of wild oranges and palmetto cabbages. This everyday scene touched John Hawk and made him reflect on the precious freedom he had come so recently to take for granted. No man could lay the lash on him. No man could sell him. And he was aware that he and Osceola were speaking better English all the time.

When Osceola and Wild Cat returned with their impressive catch of fish, they brought with them a small bunch of sticks, dyed red with beet juice. Wild Cat handed the sticks to John Hawk, and both Indians roared with laughter. When John asked what was so funny, Osceola said between chuckles, "You're the chosen mate of Wild Cat's twin!"

John looked around for confirmation from Chumpee, but she was busy fixing the fire and unaware of the joke. That night, before he fell asleep, John pictured life as the brave who protected beautiful Chumpee, daughter of King Philip. Would that make him a prince? Married to Chumpee, a man would feel like a prince. Someday, he thought, he would marry her. Someday. Osceola had once told him that a black man could become an Indian chief. Nothing in his life would please him more, John thought, than to be a Seminole chief.

At dawn of that torrid July day, John was awakened by sounds of excitement and terror. He hurried from the cell-like room he had been sharing with Osceola. But Osceola was nowhere about. The women were running to gather up children and round up horses from the nearby hammocks. Chumpee dragged a cow and a basket of fruit into the storehouse. John rushed to help her. "What's going on?"

"Boats upriver! Navy's attackin' us!"

"The United States Navy?" John thought she must have gone mad. Why would the United States Navy be in Spanish Territory?

His stomach jumped into his throat. He thought he would vomit. There stood Osceola, his face distorted with fury. John rushed to him, "What's going on?"

"An Indian runner says the navy's comin' to retake slaves."

"Oh, come on, Osceola," John cried in a voice he hardly recognized as his own. "This is Spanish country. You begged me to come here."

"I never begged!" Osceola, even in fear, would not be accused of begging. Wild Cat, wearing a straw hat, led the cows into the fort. He left the huge gate open. At home in King Philip's village, no one ever worried about an open gate. With a cry of anguish, Osceola leapt to lock the gate. John Hawk studied the thick walls. Could an enemy get through them? He had felt secure and safe when he came. Only last night, Chumpee and Wild Cat had talked with John Hawk about settling here and making a family.

As Osceola raised his frightened voice in the Seminole alert, *Yo-ho-heeee*, a familiar cold shiver ran down John's spine. As many as could get up the ladders, men with their bows and arrows, their black bodies gleaming naked to the waist, scrambled to the roof of the fort. Some gazed in moody stares that belied fear. Others looked out of frankly frightened faces, the whites of their eyes enormous. The Apalachicola River shone like glass in the blazing sun.

Nothing moved in the sheltered forest save a palm leaf or a flitting bird. In the heavy humid air, not a sound rose. Then a cow mooed, wanting to be milked. The children were unnaturally quiet, hardly breathing. The fort held an ominous still-ness of pure terror. On the river, a long sleepy alligator stirred. John had begun to doubt the truth of the runner's message when a canoe came into view, paddled by two hardmuscled Indians. John rushed to open the gates. The Indians had brought a woven basket full of muskets and ammunition.

"Powder!" Micanopy jumped out of the canoe, saying, "Whole damn navy comin' upriver."

Osceola welcomed Micanopy. Strangely calm now, Osceola assured his friend that the British had left a good powder sup-ply. Osceola assessed the protection of the walls of the fort, while Micanopy showed John Hawk how to load the powder into one of the muskets he had brought. John Hawk had longed for a gun of his own, but he would have preferred a bet-ter time for learning to use it.

The fort resounded with the firing of the rifles. John Hawk wondered if runaways might have a chance against two gun-boats, two schooners, and a supply ship acomin'. Never.

Of the more than 300 Indians and blacks in the fort, none had ever fired a shot at a man. Some of the blacks were expe-rienced marksmen because of their hunting. John worried about facing the navy gunboats and trained fighters. With an eagerness born of desperation, every man took up a gun. Chumpee insisted she wanted a musket. When she pulled the trigger, she cried out in pain, "My shoulder! That hurt!"

John Hawk loaded and fired, aiming at a knothole. He was-n't even close. Concentrating, he kept trying.

The women cooked cabbage and beet soup and roasted fish. As dusk fell, the people of the fort gathered around the fire to tell stories of slavery, of beatings, of lost parents, or bitter win-ters without clothing. "We will never be taken back to slav-ery," one old man promised.

John Hawk ate, but he hardly tasted the food. He hurried back to the roof. From that vantage point, he was the first to call out that the gunboats were approaching, three ominous black silhouettes on the horizon, with swinging, lighted lanterns. So little did the navy expect opposition, the boats announced their presence with lighted lamps. Dark clouds hid the moon in a purple sky.

Sliding down from the rough wall of the fort, John Hawk signaled the women and children to leave by the underground tunnel that had been used for potato storage in the barn. The tunnel led out from the landside of the fort wall. The people would be able to hide in the tropical forest.

John Hawk held both his father's ax and the unfamiliar musket. An old man sang:

> Before I stay in hell one day,
> Heaven shall be-a my home,
> I sing and pray my soul away,
> Heaven shall be-a my home.

Around the fort, armed men cried, "Amen, Amen, Heaven's to be-a free!"

The husky crooning voice rose again. Chumpee, close to John Hawk, sang in her sweet girl's voice. John, touched to his core, joined the song. He promised himself that if they both came through this terrible day alive, he would someday marry Chumpee.

> Good news, mister! Good news, member!
> Don't you mind what Satan say,
> Good news, members, good news!
> I heard what Heaven say today . . .
>
> Osceola have a home in Paradise,
> Brought us warnin's to use our eyes
> Good news, member, good news . . .

How often John had heard that song in which friends were praised for a good deed, for bagging a turkey or a deer, for rescuing a child from the river, for celebrating a marriage. Now, for the first time, he heard his own name sung in the song:

John Hawk have a home in Paradise,
Shootin' a gun in the fray . . .
He know good how to pray . . .
John Hawk heard Heaven speak today!

On the roof, the men watched the gunboats sail closer, closer, now almost within firing distance of Negro Fort. John Hawk knew the outlines of the ships by heart: two gunboats, two schooners, a supply ship. All were menacing, bearing down like wild animals on their prey. John Hawk sang to give himself courage, a song his mother had taught him when he was a little child sharing her cabin. She had warned him not to sing it when others were around. He thought he had forgotten the words, but suddenly, both tune and words came to mind, and he heard himself singing as if in a dream: 0, freedom! Freedom!

0, freedom over me.
Before I'd be a slave,
I'd be buried in my grave,
And go home to my Lord
and be free!

John Hawk sang alone, his voice low and vibrant. Then the old man who had saluted John with such a tender tribute joined in. Then the women and children, and finally everyone seemed to join in. The fort echoed with the song as if it were a church hymn: "O, freedom! 0, freedom!"

In John's voice was his mother's tone of patience and endurance. But his mood was not resignation. He felt a strong determination, a mood of life urgency. He felt the song to be a spiraling aspiration, a lifting, soaring sound of pure passion. The people sang with conviction, "And be free!"

The song was a prayer, ended by a fearful explosion. *Boom! Boom! Boom!!!* The fort, struck by dozens of fired cannons, echoed and reechoed under fierce fire. Batteries sent the screaming, frightened birds out of the trees. Maimed and dead birds and feathers fell everywhere. From the parapet, John heard the terrified women and children screaming and crying.

Boom! Boom! Boom! The cannons roared.

"Chumpee, take the babies and mothers and go through that potato tunnel—quick. Quick!" John Hawk ordered. He helped Chumpee up and pushed an infant into her arms. "Go!"

Cannon balls landed on the wall directly beneath the armed men. The timbers of the fort trembled but held. The wall was well-built, solid. John patted the barricade beneath him as if it were a living horse. These walls had been home to blacks and Indians. Here he had been accepted unquestiongly, the women as mothers, the men as fathers, all were brothers and sisters. Family. Tribesmen. It was over too soon.

The booming thunder of cannons rent the air horribly. Children screamed, wailed. Below him, John Hawk saw that a cannon had found its mark in a family. A boy lay across his bleeding, moaning mother, hitting her face with dark, pudgy hands, crying, "Wake up, Mama!"

John Hawk slid down the barricade wall and lifted the child in his arms as a cannon ball exploded within a few feet of him. The earth broke and threw upward sand and dirt and splintered wood.

Around John Hawk, groans of the wounded and dying mixed with the noise of the whistling and exploding of the many ships' steady firing. With the boy in his arms, John cried, "Let's make a break for it!"

Above the shrieking and crying, John Hawk heard voices from the sailors on the ship, "Loomis, fire up another!"

John Hawk suddenly saw Horrible Hortense on the ground, blood gushing out of her head. She was only a visitor to the fort, a woman who had lost her young husband in an accident at sea, whose whole fate seemed to be tragic. She was dying. Hortense, who had wanted to be called Evening Star, cried out, "No, no." And she died.

Osceola's cry pierced the air, *"Yo-ho-heeeeeee!"* It was a sig-

nal for the people to evacuate the fort. Already the walls were in flames. Though men on the roof still aimed their muskets, it was in vain, as if a kitten were trying to fight off a cougar.

John Hawk, fighting through flame, smoke, and falling timbers, ran to the storage bin. Flames swept around the stockade and raced through dry woven baskets and stacked kindling. Higher than the trees, the flames shot up like living devils.

Again came Osceola's warning, "*Yo-ho-heeeeeee!*" John Hawk held the boy hard and tight against his chest and ran through the kitchen, urging Chumpee and Wild Cat and an old woman ahead of him. "Go! Go! Get out of here!" His nose and throat scorched with smoke, his skin blistered by heat, he pushed people through the low opening in the potato bin into the dark cool sand and mud tunnel. He wet a rag to put over the boy's mouth and nose and then crawled through the waisthigh, airless tunnel, pushing and shoving until he emerged outside the burning fort among those who had gone on ahead.

Smoke and flames turned the fort into an inferno. Hardly had he left the stockade when a red-hot cannon ball fired with a heavy charge landed on the Negro Fort powder magazine. The roof collapsed with the boom of a hundred cannons.

Banked beyond the stream, canoes with paddles waited like sleeping alligators. Seminole canoes carved from cypress trees were large enough to carry twenty or thirty people. Into these boats crowded the survivors of Blount's Fort. Children and old people lay on the floor of the canoes. Osceola shoved off first, stealthily, silently, hardly making a sound on the river. The line of canoes followed, with paddles dipping as softly as the river lapped the shore. Behind them, cannon fire continued. The noise intensified even as the canoes moved from shore.

Escape now depended on luck. The people of Blount's Fort had had very little luck this night. Not a family remained intact. Most of those in the canoes were the sole survivors of their family. The canoes slipped along beneath the overhanging shelter of willows in the midnight dark. Clouds promised rain hid the moon and stars. The cannon fire boomed and boomed, exploding an awful violence. The children were as quiet as death. Smoke and flames from the fort blackened the sky. The wind carried the smell of scorch and death down the river to the runaways.

Seminole canoes carried the burned, the injured, the terrorized people who had been hit by falling timbers or bits of exploding cannon metal or burning wood. Osceola, John Hawk, Micanopy, Chumpee, Wild Cat, and many children were in the lead canoe.

Miles from the destroyed fort, the exhausted refugees pulled their boats into a hidden tropical inlet. As they got out, their feet sank ankle-deep in marsh and mud. The canoes were dragged into the jungle and covered with tree branches. Leaves of trees were rearranged to hide any sign of where they had come ashore.

As the sun rose, tropical birds raised a song; how could the birds know this was not a dawn for singing? Just before noon, from their hiding place in the deep thicket, the refugees spotted the gunboats sailing by. On the deck of the first gunboat, those people of Negro Fort who had been captured were in chains. John Hawk, struck with a rush of anger and agony, pity and frustration, cried aloud. Chumpee cried too. Osceola admonished her, "We will rescue them. Don't cry."

John Hawk longed to protect Chumpee, to save her from all tragedy. "Chumpee!" he said with a tenderness he hardly knew he had in him. At the sound of her name spoken so compassionately, she began to cry even harder. Osceola again scolded her, "Indian women do not cry!"

Chumpee rubbed her eyes with the back of her hand ruefully. With great effort, she controlled her sobs.

"There's a brave girl," John delivered the ultimate compliment.

John lay on his stomach, burying his face in his arms, feeling his skin scorched, tight, burned. He smelled the damp, sweet grass and the tiny wildflowers crushed beneath his nose.

He recognized the flower as an Indian herb medicine. Lifting his head, he saw the old black woman treating her burns with wet leaves and poultices made from the flower. John rose wearily to his knees and reached around to gather handfuls of the herb. He rolled it in his palms and patted it on his face. Immediately, his skin felt less taut, less painful. He gathered more of the herb, dipped it in the river edge, and covered a child's burned legs with it.

He saw Chumpee's arms, scorched and burning red, her neck blistered. With a poultice of wet leaves and flowers, he softly patted her arms. Then he found a thin vine and tied the leaves around her neck like a collar. The little white flowers seemed pretty around her slender neck.

"That feels better," Chumpee said. She managed a smile. John Hawk, his throat scorched, had trouble swallowing.

When night fell, the people slept. Osceola woke up John Hawk from a sleep of exhaustion. "We're not far from Pacheco's plantation," Osceola said. "I've got to get food and help. A friend of mine named Luis lives there. I'm leaving now."

"I'll go too."

"No, a man alone may get through unnoticed. A Seminole is safer than a black."

John Hawk rose and dug two baked potatoes out of the coals of a low fire. Gazing around at the sleeping refugees, he wondered if he would ever again see Chumpee and her twin, Wild Cat. He was determined to go with Osceola. Life seemed savage — hard. He felt a desperate love for Chumpee, for life itself, despite its difficulties. He had a slow, gnawing doubt about leaving the safety of the group to venture through the jungle. The snakes, mosquitoes, alligators, and wild animals were bad enough. The slave catchers were worse.

In the fort, he had known a moment when death seemed to put a hand on him. He had known the awesome idea of "forever." His throat was scorched raw with despair, smoke, fatigue. Nothing would keep him from going with Osceola.

Blount's Fort had not been called Indian Fort; it had been known as Negro Fort.

He remembered the story Osceola had told about the braves who drew sticks. The one who got the red stick went on the mission. Only a few days ago, John had been teased with a bundle of red sticks to suggest that he would marry Chumpee. But now, John himself would choose the red stick as a sign that he was volunteering to go into danger.

5

John Hawk, feeling hopeless and homeless, followed a roughly sketched map on doeskin. He made his way downstream toward Fort Brooke, the white man's military stockade. Barefoot, carrying his rough sandals, he waded the narrow part of the stream. In an orange grove, he stopped to pick some ripe fruit.

Near the rutted road marked with an X on his map, he would come upon the plantation belonging to Antonio Pacheco. John would know it by the large white house and the number of barns. Osceola had warned John Hawk to come by the rear near the slave quarters. There he would ask for Luis, who had the same last name of his master, Pacheco.

"This Luis is a slave, the son of the master, like you," Osceola had confided. "He speaks Spanish like a Spaniard, English like a gentleman. He was born in Washington. He understands Seminole and French. He's in good with his father. He will get us food and horses so we can get back to Cuscowilla."

The idea of riding a horse made John's heart beat faster.

Ever since he was a little fellow on his father's plantation, he had watched the overseer mounted on a beautiful stallion, trotting about like a prince, high above everyone else. Envy of the overseer now turned to desire, and John hoped against hope he would one day own a horse of his own.

The sun rose. Radiant clouds, outlined in gold, floated in

the new sky, streaked with pink and purple. Spotting a shadow in the distance, John Hawk was gripped by a fever of fear. He lurked behind a thick tree trunk. The figure, small, square, slow moving, proved to be an old black woman, fat and graceless, swathed in torn garments.

"Missus!" John cried, running after her. The old woman turned in fear. "Yas, suh?"

Spotting the ax in John's hand, she reared back, terrorized. "You fixin' to kill me?"

"No, no," he quickly reassured her, "I be seekin' Pacheco's place."

"Luis Pacheco?"

John nodded, and the old woman pointed in the direction from which she had come, "He be in that barn."

John peered through the thick tropical forest. Indeed, there ahead of him were the roofs of the buildings, the big house, the barns, the slave quarters. The old woman trotted off with greater alacrity than John would have suspected she had in her. He wished he had not startled her.

As he approached the open door of the whitewashed barn, here came a young black his own age, about thirteen, shorter than John, darker.

"Luis Pacheco?" asked John.

The young man's eyebrows rose inquisitively. "Lucky guess," was the reply. The youth's face seemed carved of coal. John hesitated to offer his hand, but Luis took the initiative. They shook hands, formally, introducing themselves, and John explained his mission. Luis agreed to help. He was already aware of the survivors of Blount's Fort.

Luis studied John. "You could pass for a white man. Where did you get that name, John Hawk?"

John said his name had been White, but the sight of a hawk had inspired him to change his name. "I been in flight since," John attempted a joke.

Luis smiled, revealing huge white perfect teeth. "I can give you bags of yam, dried beans, corn. How many survivors?'"

"Fifty. Some very sick, some badly burned."

"A guy named Carson from the Fort got here a few hours ago. He's badly burned. We have some oil for burns I'll give you. Carson says few in the Fort survived, hundreds died. Some blacks were taken prisoner on the ships, but no Indians."

John Hawk wondered about Carson's facts. Indians did not like to admit they were taken alive. The philosophy was to fight to the death. He grieved for his brothers recaptured to slavery.

John, eyeing a beautiful stallion, wished he dared ask for the horse. But Luis was already saddling up an old nag. John helped him tie up bags of beans, yams, potatoes, carrots, and corn to the saddle. Luis swung a side of bacon into a hemp bag and laced the drawstrings of the bag around the old leather saddle.

"You won't get in trouble for giving away this horse?" John wondered aloud.

"Naw," Luis reassured him, "ain't gonna miss this old nag. He only good for giving the white kids rides. The kids call him Sugar."

John Hawk scraped a carrot clean with the sharp edge of his father's ax. Sitting on an overturned barrel, he chewed on the carrot. The horse brought his head down to nudge John Hawk, and John fed him the last inch of carrot. How John longed for a horse of his own. Someday he would have one.

"You ain't a slave, Luis?" asked John.

Luis considered his reply. "Slavery here is different from the States. This here's Spanish territory. Spanish law goes by Catholics, and the Church hates slavery."

John Hawk listened to those words as if they were a lesson. The Spanish system was like half a loaf being better than none, or a little freedom being better than nothing. You had a taste, you wanted more.

"How do it differ, slavery here in Spanish territory?" John pressed Luis, who looked back at him oddly, huge black eyes flashing.

"Here slaves marry," Luis replied. "You marry, you can't be separated from your wife. A master can't have his way with a wife or a daughter. A slave can buy freedom."

John challenged, "You gonna buy yours?"

"My master will free me when I am forty."

John thought of age forty as next to never. That black boy's gotta behave for a long time. John did not say it aloud. "How old be you?"

"Seventeen."

"You talk fine English."

"I talk fine in four-five languages."

"Not braggin' a'course," John said.

Slaves carrying jars of honey, pails of milk, baskets of eggs, and fruit hurried toward the big house. Luis patted a child on the head and lifted an orange from the basket of a slave to give to the black child. He offered a lovely girl his bigtoothed smile. Luis seemed more mature than John Hawk, more in control of his life. John, jealous, wanted to imitate Luis's self-confidence and manners. He wished he knew a language other than English.

"Stay here," Luis ordered, "I'm gonna get you somethin' from the master's lodge."

The old horse was so laden now that John wondered-if the nag could carry him as well as all the provisions. He fed another carrot to the nag; the animal ate gratefully. He walked the nag to a watering place, where the horse drank thirstily.

Soon Luis returned with a loaf of fresh bread and a small goatskin of milk. "Drink some milk and take the rest to the kids. If it sours, it can be rested for cheese."

John tried to thank him.

"Save it!" Luis said like a man. "Get going." They shook hands again, and John knew he had made a friend.

He had come through the woods in predawn dark, studying his rough map every foot of the way. In broad daylight, John led the nag through heavy underbrush and junglelike forest.

"Get along, Sugar," John Hawk urged gruffly, feeling foolish about his sudden affection for the old nag. He would like to settle down somewhere, have a horse, farm a piece of land, be a man like Luis. When he delivered the grub to the refugees, he could take the nag back to the plantation and ask to work there. Not as a slave, but as a paid worker. The horse came to the stream that had to be forded, and he hesitated. John allowed the horse to drink. He himself splashed his face and neck with cold water and had a good drink. His skin, now healing, the blisters gone, still felt taut and itchy.

Leading the horse by the strings of the bags of beans, he was pleased that Sugar obediently followed him, lifting a proud head up and down and picking his way across the stream.

All afternoon, John kept the hot sun at his back, repeatedly checking his rough map on doeskin. His mind turned often to what Luis had said, "Slavery here is different." How could Luis tolerate slavery until he was forty? Freedom at forty! Half a lifetime spent in bondage. A man could buy his freedom. Surely indebtedness was better than slavery.

John Hawk sniffed. He smelled the sea and knew he was not too far now from where the refugees were camped. Through the trees, he spotted a thin sliver of smoke rising above the treetops. That should be it. The camp. At last.

Through a narrow clearing, Osceola came running. "What took so long?"

John laughed, "It seemed a short decade to me."

The women unloaded the food and with quick, trembling hands set bacon frying over the open pit fire, crisscrossed with green sticks. Potatoes, carrots, and corn were wrapped with wild onions in palmetto leaves which the women had gathered. The little rolls were thrust into the hot coals. Chumpee took oranges from the branches and cut the fruit into quarters, handing everyone a share.

Soon the air was fragrant with boiling sassafras bark tea. The children helped. The preparation of the meal promised renewal and hope. The men ate first; then, passing a corncob pipe among themselves, smoked whatever dried weeds the women had picked for the elders. The pipe, passed from hand to hand, had a sharp fragrance. The men planned the expedition back to Cuscowilla. After the women and children ate, the babies were bedded down in piles of leaves.

John was pleased that in his absence doeskin litters had been made ready for the wounded. The women, wasting no time, had sewn together rags and ends of hides to make bags to carry food and to shape cradles that could swing across shoulders for children too small to walk. The women had built shelters of green sticks and branches. When a soft rain fell that night, the refugees were comfortably dry under the shelters.

In the morning, only two of the wounded would admit to needing stretchers. They were the old men. Gently, they were lifted to the stretched doeskin. Little boys peed on the fire. The mothers buried the last embers and piled green leaves on the pits to hide evidence of where the camp had been. A wild melon was cut into tiny pieces so that every child had a thin slice.

Now the survivors, each carrying an end of a litter, a baby, or a sack of food, followed single-file behind Osceola and John Hawk. John felt a pang of pride to be in the lead; he was recognized as a brave, a responsible member of the Seminoles. He had no cause to envy Luis Pacheco. But he did envy Luis the knowledge of languages, and a place where he belonged. Drawing up the end of the long line was Sugar, with an injured man astride, and many bags of leftover food. The old man's head rested on his chest, dejected because he could not walk on burned feet.

As the caravan moved at an easy pace through wild orange groves, Chumpee brought a bunch of sweet-smelling flowers to John Hawk. "Are these the flowers you use to salve burns?" she asked.

"No, I use wild poppies." She picked some orange, red, and yellow stalks and asked, "What are these then?"

"Indian paintbrush." At least he knew that.

Later she brought him a little yellow feather. "What kind of bird did this come from?" How should he know? He gave her a playful push, embarrassed at questions he could not answer. Later she found an egg shell. He knew it belonged to a grackle and was pleased to be able to say so. He studied the little yellow feather. It could be from a wild canary, he said.

"You know everything!" she said, inappropriately, her eyes trusting, perhaps flirtatious.

He laughed. "Acourse I do!"

At nightfall, the mood was heavier. The runaways worried about their reception when they would get to Cuscowilla. Mounting anxiety spread as they came to a clearing. Aware that the women were exhausted, Osceola called a halt. The women wearily untied bags of food and the girls gathered mushrooms, wild oranges, wild squash, sassafras bark, and cabbage leaves full of berries. Still, supper was meager for fifty people.

At daybreak, Osceola poked John, saying, "Let's go fishing." John felt stiff, his legs aching. Osceola had fashioned two rough fishing rods and they ran, John with his ax, down to the water's edge. Lying on their backs as the sun rose, they let their lines play beneath the still water. Only birds, snakes, and fish moved. Behind them, the sleeping refugees, covered by piles of leaves, scarcely stirred.

Squawking and singing, a whole flock of great white herons with impressive wing spreads (as wide as a man is long) swooped majestically across the blue white of the morning sky. The immaculate whiteness of the herons accented by yellow-green bills and legs was a sight to lift John's spirits. Cawing and crying, the herons swept down for fish.

"They're getting our breakfast," Osceola complained sourly as a heron carried away a beakful of fish.

"Oh, go on!" John laughed, lifting his fish switch with its

hook in the mouth of a giant bass.

"Great going!" exclaimed Osceola. "Look! I got one too." Not to be outdone, he lifted his line and up came the fish huge, fighting, struggling. Osceola threw the switch to the ground and himself on top of the enormous bass, clutching the fish frantically in both hands.

"I got him! I got him!" he cried, as if to reassure himself as the fish fought to get free. John plunged a long, sharp-pointed green stick through the squirming fish.

Luckily, John's bass was not so belligerent. Quickly, both fish were speared and soon were roasting on spits over a hot fire. The sweet, sharp fragrance of the cooking fish brought the children out of their sacks of leaves to a circle from which they poked small twigs into the fire.

The last of Luis's potatoes had baked overnight in hot coals. Chumpee offered the children palmetto leaves full of berries, and soon all their mouths were circled with dark red juice.

"What a great breakfast!" Osceola exulted.

John remembered those rare mornings when his Aunt Sara had made him buttermilk pancakes with leftover batter in his father's kitchen. There had been syrup too. He was suddenly homesick for his father's plantation and for a sight of his mother. He missed her. It had been two long years since he had seen her.

Late in the day, the weary band of refugees from Blount's Fort came at last to Cuscowilla. The children of the hammock were at the outskirts of the field, whooping and hollering, clapping together pieces of wood to scare off crows and jackdaws. The old man on Sugar slid off the horse and, as his feet hit the grass, he collapsed. When John Hawk rushed to him, he realized the old man was dead.

Despite their weariness, two elderly refugees lifted the dead man with infinite tenderness and carried his body to the nearest chickee. Cabbage leaves were brought to cover the dead man's face. The Indians of Cuscowilla gathered round and sang a burial song. Then they welcomed the refugees and made them feel at home.

6

Word had reached Cuscowilla of the destruction of Blount's Fort. The Seminoles had been wild with worry about their kin, but they hid their emotions. Osceola's mother presented a quiet face as she took John Hawk's hand. "Come, share our chickee," she said.

John felt relief at being back in the hammock home of the Seminoles. He knew many of the people who lived in the thirty elevated cottages. Shaded with open platforms reached by portable ladders, each cottage had a room for cooking and a room for sleeping, one above the other. In the open upper room, men received guests. Here the family slept in the warm, open air all year round.

Each family had a garden with corn, beans, tobacco, melons, yams. A large fertile plantation was farmed by the village women and children. A fence kept out the animals.

Now the refugees were led to the center of the plantation, where a common storage building held grain and food. Hadjo told the refugees to take all they needed. The supplies represented a tax that the villagers paid to provide for the old, the ill, or runaway slaves. "You be welcome," Hadjo said.

The medicine man treated burns and ailments of the refugees. Hospitality eased the misery of homelessness. The women piled wood on the fire. Hunters brought a deer which the women skinned. Chumpee stretched the deerskin to dry.

Soon the meat was roasting on a spit above a huge fire. Osceola's mother cooked the deer liver over her own fire and Chumpee, Wild Cat, John Hawk, and Osceola shared the family meal. It was a special treat.

John Hawk looked up from the good meal to see an unfamiliar Indian couple on horseback.

"My parents!" Chumpee exclaimed, jumping up to run toward them. King Philip and his wife had come to Cuscowilla, for the news of the massacre at Blount's Fort had reached them too.

King Philip, overjoyed to find his children unharmed, thanked Osceola for the family's hospitality. Chumpee said they were indebted to John Hawk. King Philip lit his pipe, inhaled the smoke, and passed the pipe to John Hawk. John Hawk was flattered, for an Indian rarely passed a peace pipe to a boy. He drew on the stem, and for a moment felt dizzy and almost ill.

That night, the Indians danced and sang. Chumpee, in the light of the fire, did a lovely slow dance. Her body, beginning to take on womanly curves, gracefully moved like palm leaves in the wind. With a warm, involved joy, John Hawk watched her dancing, and thought her as delicate and beautiful as a flowering peach tree. Her skin was the color of honey, golden smooth, and her rosy lips seemed to glow.

When she came and sat by him, John admonished her, "Why did you tell your father you owed your life to me? That's not true!"

"I believe you saved my life, John Hawk. I'm making you a jacket from the deerskin."

King Philip, leading a handsome, prancing stallion, approached John Hawk. Chumpee's father held up his hand. The drummers and the dancers and all the villagers listened respectfully.

King Philip said, "This horse is a gift to John Hawk for saving the lives of the children of King Philip."

By now, John knew that a gift from an Indian was never refused. But he was flabbergasted, his head whirling with joy and confusion. Why should he be rewarded with a splendid horse for doing his duty? He patted the horse's head. Immediately, the animal seemed to bow and acknowledge John as his master. John had to blink fast to keep tears from his eyes. Here was the most beautiful horse he had ever seen, the finest gift he could imagine.

He took the leather cord by which King Philip had led the horse, jumped on the bare back of the horse, and trotted around the open clearing. His heart was high, his happiness boundless. Beneath a full, glowing moon, he felt like a prince in a story. He, who had been a slave and had owned nothing more than a pocketknife, a book, and an ax, was now a free man on a beautiful horse.

For the next few days, John Hawk, with Osceola's guidance, trained the horse to walk quietly beneath him, to respond to his commands, to trot, to run, to gallop, to turn. John had never been so happy in his life. A horse of his own. He felt rich.

He watched Chumpee working on the jacket she was making for him. Honey of the bee, he thought. Her name was appropriate.

John longed to know her better. She seemed to him to glisten with an uncanny golden fire. Near her, he felt strong and manly, and full of the desire to live.

But the tall and handsome King Philip left with his family to return to his own plantation, and John missed Chumpee. Not even the beautiful horse could make up for Chumpee's absence.

7

Two years had passed since John Hawk had seen Chumpee or Wild Cat. Secure and at home now in Cuscowilla, he regarded everyone in the hammock as family.

In August, Luis's father gave Luis a week off with permission to visit Cuscowilla. Luis and John Hawk had the time to fish, to hunt, to lie on their backs and watch the wind rustle the leaves of the palmetto trees.

Together they rode Sam around the plantation, or took turns trotting him on the dry, dusty roads nearby.

Near her chickee, Morning Dew boiled jelly from the root of the China briar. While she chopped, pounded, mixed, and strained the jelly, Luis read from Spanish newspapers, translating into English for John, Osceola, and Morning Dew. Andrew Jackson had defeated the Creek Indians and imposed a treaty sharper than an ax. Even those Creeks who had helped Jackson win were forced to give up their lands.

"The trouble is," Luis observed, "Jackson thinks Indians are all alike. He thinks Indians are all one big tribe."

Osceola agreed. "Now many Creeks will come to Spanish Florida. They will meet hatred here."

"Right," Luis concurred.

Hadjo walked toward them through the pastoral scene of children playing, dogs, and cattle. Horses stood around like knights on a chessboard. Hadjo wore a cap, a *co-to-po-kaa*, and a breech cloth called *e-kof-kaw* in the Indian tongue. Hadjo meant "fearless courage." The Seminoles name a man for bravery in war. A boy would have a "baby name" until he earned a title in battle. Seminole men customarily did manual work like women until they proved themselves warriors. John Hawk had yet to see a mature Indian man work the fields or take care of the cattle. The men rode and groomed the horses.

Hadjo asked Luis about the news.

"The Spanish papers," Luis replied, "report that if Jackson comes to Florida, the Spanish will consider that an act of war."

Later that day, taking up two rifles, John and Luis went through open pasture. Along a shaded path in the forest, they entered junglelike shade, the palmetto leaves closing out the hot sun. Snakes and little green lizards slithered through fallen leaves and dead branches. On a rotting tree limb, a tiny chipmunk scolded them for disturbing the peace. John Hawk aimed his rifle at the chattering chipmunk, then thought better of it. Let the little thing live, he decided. There was not enough food or fur to it to waste a bullet.

Luis signaled for them to separate. John went to the right, through an opening in the underbrush. There two wild turkey gobblers fed. The turkeys either saw or felt the youth's presence. Fluttering their wings, they lifted into the darkness of the forest, disappearing before John could take aim. Missing his footing, John fell into a muddy marsh. Before he realized what was happening, he was in quicksand up to his knees. He hadn't been so terrified since the attack on Blount's Fort.

"Luis!" he cried. "Help!"

The panic in his voice gave him a moment of shame. He conquered his fear to try to catch the branch of a tree well out of his reach. He grasped only a weak, thin, leafy branch. When he tried to drag it down to pull himself upward, the branch broke. How was he going to get out of this sucking, stinking quicksand? His struggles only made him go deeper into the mire.

Now buried waist deep, feeling his legs being pulled downward, he dragged at weeds and the roots of a tree. His hands were torn by thorns. His heart pumped so hard he thought if he didn't drown in the quicksand, his chest would break open.

Up to his armpits in the thick, mucky clay, he shouted, "Help! Luis! Help!"

Off in the distance, a crack of a rifle might mean Luis shot an animal or a bird and would be engrossed in fetching it. He would not hear John's cries for help. Or maybe Luis was beyond earshot.

Panic was an emotion John Hawk refused to accept. Struggling to get out of the slime and sand only made him sink deeper. He told himself, "Don't give up!" He had been in worse messes than this. At the moment he could not think of any. He bit his lip until the blood ran down his chin. Surrounded by sharp sawgrass that would tear his hands to pieces if he grasped it, he eyed the miserably thorny weeds within reach. Now only his arms, hands, and head were free of the sucking mud. But he could still reach the rifle that was on a little grassy mound.

He took hold of the gun and placed it over the quagmire, bracing himself on it and feeling strength in his arms as he pushed down on the gun. Inch by difficult inch, he managed to lift his heavy mud-encrusted body. Every ounce of willpower and energy went into lifting himself. He had his chest out of the mud. Then he was out of it up to his waist. With great effort, he could pull one leg up and get his knee on the rifle.

He dragged the other heavy mud-covered leg upward, sucking it up through the wet sand, hoping against hope the ends of the rifle would remain firmly on solid earth on each side of the marshy hole. Now, with the other leg out of the sand, he knelt in a balancing act, breathing hard as if he had run a long distance. He rested a moment to ready himself to thrust his body to the grassy dry mound. With a great force of energy, he pushed his thighs and arms and threw himself past the cutting sawgrass which tore the flesh from his face. He lay on the hard, brush-covered ground, his heart pounding, too tired to move.

Luis, with his rifle in one hand, a red and black feathered turkey in the other, came upon John. He stared at John Hawk's mud-coated body and bleeding face.

"Catch anything?" he asked.

"Caught cold," John managed.

8

John Hawk had been at Cuscowilla five years by the time he and Luis had another holiday together. Both young men, tall and muscular, were skilled riders and bursting with self confidence.

Luis had an errand in St. Augustine for his master. He arrived at Cuscowilla with two passes signed by Gen. Wiley Thompson, the Indian agent at Fort King. Without such a pass, no Indian or black man could be on the streets of St. Augustine.

John, always eager for adventure, offered Luis a new canoe the Seminoles had made from a cypress tree. John and Luis filled it with tanned furs, deerskins, and doeskins that could be traded in St. Augustine. Morning Dew gave John some roast chicken, corn, and little potatoes.

The two young men, strong and eager, managed the canoe easily between them, despite the long portage. Luis talked a blue streak.

"St. Augustine is the oldest city in the New World. Ships been comin' here since 1565."

"You a walkin' history book," John said sarcastically. But, in truth, he was impressed by Luis, and ashamed of his own ignorance. A slave as knowledgeable as Luis was rare.

They reached the shore. The tides were with them. The canoe sped effortlessly on the briskly running waves, the blades dipping rhythmically, smoothly. John and Luis made a good pair, their strokes well matched.

The land along the shore was mostly white beach and beyond it, uncleared forests. Then the roofs of a small town became visible. Already, St. Augustine magnetized travelers who wished to escape cold northern winters.

Luis explained with a bitter chuckle, "Newspapers predict a flourishing business here in oranges, lumber, tar, and turpentines. Acourse, it gotta wait until them blacks and Indians is driven out."

After a few hours of paddling the canoe, John Hawk saw two-story buildings with hand-hewn beams, and signs that read "HOTEL."

Luis said, "Hotel for whites only."

St. Augustine lay like a magic mirage in the sunset. Small boats bobbed on white breakers where the Atlantic Ocean poured through a narrow inlet into the bay. Lanterns on a distant ship glowed like stars against the twilight sky. Dusk: John's favorite time of day. Everything seemed softened in the half-light. The lanterns bobbed, disappearing and reappearing, as the canoe rode the rollers which carried it over a shallow bar.

John, spotting a great massive fort ahead, asked, "Luis, what's that?"

"That's Castillo de San Marcos."

"Spanish?"

"You bet it's Spanish. And unconquerable."

What a great word, John thought, saying it silently, "Unconquerable!"

John could believe those walls were unconquerable. The fort — huge, square, thick — seemed impenetrable.

"They say no one ever escaped from San Marcos."

"What's that stuff it's built of?"

"Coquina . . . shells."

"Shells?!!"

"Surprised you! The Spanish quarry it from Anastasia Island.

Coquina's made from shells glued by lime and time." Luis, his arms tired from handling the paddle, continued, "Coquina's easy to quarry and shape. They say a cannon ball fired at a thick coquina wall like that will bounce off like a ball."

John, recalling the destruction at Blount's Fort, was impressed. Luis misread John's expression and thought that John was impressed by his erudition. Luis, a little vain, since few slaves even knew how to read or write one language, let alone four or five, said he hoped someday to be a teacher.

"What would you teach?"

"I could teach Spanish, French, English, maybe history. I could teach the Seminole language to whites."

The canoe topped a wave, and John had an excellent view of the fort, sitting like four connected castles behind a ditch.

"See that slope," Luis pointed, "that's a glacis! A detached area defends the gate. Wait 'til you see them Grenada oranges! Lemons and limes and pomegranates and figs grow in St. Augustine!" he exclaimed enthusiastically.

John lifted his paddle, letting a strong, white-capped wave carry the canoe ashore. Hot and sweaty, they beached the canoe beneath a palm tree. Stripping, they ran into the rough surf. The white-foamed waves hit them sharply, refreshingly cold. The taste of sharp salt on his lips was pleasant as John swam vigorously as far as the point where a lighthouse was being built. How good it felt to swim instead of paddle after a long day. His muscles relaxed.

Suddenly, on the crest of a wave, in the deepening dusk, he spotted something like a stick upright in the water. The dorsal fin of a shark!

A shark!

Why did his holidays with Luis turn dangerous? John, swimming frantically, turned and rode the next swiftly running wave shoreward. Caught in an undertow, he was dragged seaward again, toward the mouth of the menacing shark. In stark fear, John swallowed salt water. At once a huge wave lifted him and he saw Luis through eyes half blinded by sea water.

"Luis! Go back! Sharks!" His words, drowned by the noise of waves and wind, were repeated, "Go back!"

Luis understood the waving and the warnings. He made for shore. Both came up in shallow water together, breathless and almost doubled over in fatigue. They threw themselves onto the wet brown carpet of sand and tried to catch their breath. John vomited sea water.

"What happened?" Luis demanded.

"A shark almost got me!"

"Lot of excitement over only one shark!" Luis, shaking his head, went off to gather driftwood to build a fire. Later, he went after oysters, and returned with a deerskin full. With John's father's ax, he cracked open the oysters into a clay pot. These he set on the fire with palmetto leaves. John brought out food from the canoe.

They made beds of doeskins on the sand. All night they slept soundly. In the morning, they were awakened by a Spanish sea captain offering to buy their furs and hides. Luis bargained with him, asking twice what the Spaniard offered. But John said, "I think he offers a fair price."

John and Luis piled the furs into the captain's small skiff that would take him to his ship. The captain insisted on giving the money to John. From his pocket, the captain took a small silver crucifix fastened to a silver chain. "This comes from the mission and is blessed by a priest." He hung the silver chain around John's neck.

John thanked him. "I believe in omens, especially good ones."

"What's going on down there?" Luis asked the sea captain about a crowd of Indians.

"A beached shark. The Indians are cooking it."

Suddenly, several Indians began calling and waving, summoning John and Luis to come for breakfast. John and Luis put on doeskin pants and hurried to the crowd.

The circling waves enveloped the body of the shark, whose blood ran out to sea.

A black man introduced himself "Black Dirt," he said, "a free Spanish citizen, resident of St. Augustine, a student of law."

Luis smiled with question marks in his eyes. John, astonished that a black man could have such aspirations, said, "Luis Pacheco here speaks four languages."

Black Dirt used a knife to cut off chunks of roasted shark meat. "You say."

John liked the taste, slightly fishy, but rather like deer meat. It was better to be eating shark than having the shark eat him.

Black Dirt introduced John and Luis to the other men around the fire. Roger Goodson was a carpenter, Tony Black, a bricklayer, several were gardeners, and another a blacksmith.

Indians chopped off huge chunks of shark meat to carry to the open, airy cabins they had built—thatched roofs with cabbage palms. A number of Indian circular sentry boxes lined the beach, well back from the threat of high tides. Air holes marched up each clay and mud space between the posts. Black Dirt owned one of the sentry boxes and offered to keep the canoe for John Hawk.

That day, as John Hawk walked city streets, he felt fenced in. How confining the homes seemed to him. Each was unique, each with a little balcony providing shade for walkers. The houses, of freestone and finished with plaster, seemed solid, permanent. In the plaza, an orange tree was so heavy with fruit that the branches lay along the ground. John Hawk picked a handful of oranges, ate one, and saved the seeds. He would plant the seeds back in Cuscowilla.

St. Augustine, built in the Spanish way, formed an oblong square. Luis called it a "parallelogram." On the narrow streets, two carriages faced each other, neither with room to pass. The drivers stood on their seats, shouting, snapping their whips. Finally, in fury, the two men on the closest wagon jumped out and began pulling the wagon backward. Luis and John Hawk

59

lent a hand, dragging the wagon to clear the way for the other to turn the corner. The horses, unable to make sense of it all, whinnied and stamped their feet.

One carriage finally made it around the corner. A crowd had gathered, cheering and applauding.

In a tobacco shop, Luis bought a paper, *The East Florida Gazette*. They sat on a park bench and Luis read the advertisements: "Tuesday, 18th of July, Theatre in the State House, DOUGLAS, A TRAGEDY."

"Want to see a play?" Luis asked.

John Hawk shuddered at the idea of being closed up in a room, perhaps the only black man there. He shook his head. Sure, the idea of seeing a play excited him. But not at the risk of his life.

Luis read aloud another ad: "PUBLIC AUCTION. Thursday, next, 11 o'clock. Major Manon's quarters, a mahogany bedstead, curtains, clock, bookcase, well-toned guitar."

Below it read: "PUBLIC AUCTION TODAY . . . Negroes, cash, one comely negress."

"How can they hold an auction if blacks are free here?"

"Only runaways are exiles or refugees. If a man does not run away," Luis explained, "he is not free. Some slaves are held like property."

Luis read the news of the day, St. Augustine, July 17, 1821:

President James Monroe had appointed Andrew Jackson provisional governor of Florida. General Jackson told the press the office of governor had no appeal for him. But he had accepted the appointment because it justified his military campaigns in Florida. Mrs. Jackson, recently arrived from Pensacola, was shocked by the gaiety, dancing, and gambling in St. Augustine. She hoped her husband would put an end to such goings-on when he became governor.

Jackson refused to enter St. Augustine until the Spanish governor, José Callava, surrendered the province to the United States. Like most Spaniards, Callava moved leisurely. In any case, he was in no great hurry to turn the territory over to slave catchers. Official ceremonies of the transfer to the United States will be at ten o'clock today.

Even as Luis read the paper aloud, a burst of drum and bugle accompanied the marching beat of soldiers passing the plaza.

"Come on!" Luis urged, and he and John joined the crowd hurrying toward Government House. "That has to be Jackson!"

Sure enough, Andrew Jackson, pale and solemn, stepped down from an elegant carriage and entered Government House. Behind him, in a bouncing hoop skirt, Mrs. Jackson flounced out of the carriage. Soon the famous couple, unsmiling, appeared on a balcony high above the street. The crowd was not in a happy holiday mood. Tears stood in the eyes of many of the blacks. The Indians appeared grim, stolid, angry.

On four sides of the square, stern-faced Seminoles in moccasins and Indian garb stood by seamen with knives in their belts. Mulatto women in bright calico flirted with the sailors. Jamaican blacks wearing gold earrings carried baskets of oranges and coconuts on their heads. A fisherman peddled fish from a bucket of salt water. In *mantillas*, Spanish women escorted by handsome bearded *grandees* turned their noses up at the Indians who were selling shark meat. When Governor Callava appeared, the soldiers in sparkling military outfit snapped to attention. Callava — blond, broad-shouldered, handsome — returned their salute.

Now General Jackson walked with Callava between two lines of saluting troops — on one side, Americans, on the other, Spanish. The Fourth Infantry band played "The Star Spangled Banner." The flag of Spain fluttered to half-staff. A woman sobbed loudly.

The Stars and Stripes floated to a level with the Spanish flag and held there while in the bay, the *Hornet*, a military gunboat, boomed the first of a twenty-one-gun salute. Down came the Spanish flag. Up went the red, white, and blue, fluttering against a cloudless sky.

From where he stood, John Hawk had a view of the bay, the languorous movement of palm trees, the dip and flight of seagulls. His eye was on the fluttering Stars and Stripes. Is that my flag? My standard? Will it be good for me or bad? he wondered.

Spanish soldiers held their salute as the flag of Spain was formally folded and handed to Callava. Stillness, broken only by the cawing of the seagulls and the steady roll of the breakers against the beach, spoke of a subdued sadness. The old era passes. The new era offers uncertainty.

The Spanish soldiers marched to the waiting ships. Uneasy, Spaniards who had settled and built St. Augustine lined the sidewalks and watched their military depart. Andrew Jackson welcomed all to the freedom and democracy of the newest state in the Union, Florida.

Some blacks had soldiered for the Spanish. Many of these black men had been born free. Those born in St. Augustine when it was a Spanish province, registered from birth like any other child of any color, had felt protected. Because American policy defined all blacks as slaves, they now felt threatened.

The crowd moved en masse toward the Castillo, the Fort. Here Spanish soldiers formally brought down the Spanish flags on each of the four fortress towers; the American flag was hoisted. Sixty guns of bronze were unloaded from ships and carried to the walls to be mounted, facing the sea. Everywhere, blacks gravely worried about their future.

With the crowds, Luis and John crossed the moat over a wooden bridge into the Fort. A guard explained that the outer walls of the Fort were fourteen feet thick at the base, tapering to nine feet at the top.

"The fort was remodeled, starting in 1738. At that time, the inner wall was moved back and an arched coquina ceiling was added to all the chambers between the walls. It is impossible for anyone ever to escape from this fort."

John looked about him. He agreed that escape would be hard.

How could he know that one day he would be a prisoner here and his escape would go down in history?

9

As Luis and John Hawk strolled up St. George Street, Indians bartered venison, raccoon, squirrel, and rum, powder, and shot. John, familiar with the Indian passion for paint, beads, and bright feathers, thought he had never seen more brilliant dress. In his pouch he had Spanish coins received for the hides and furs. His first real money gave him a heady sense of power.

"Pacheco!" called a dark voice, "Luis!"

Luis turned to recognize a friend. "Micanopy!"

Micanopy, accompanied by Black Dirt, greeted John and Luis with an Indian handshake. "*Inclemas cha!*"

To John Hawk, Micanopy seemed every inch a king. His straight carriage and moccasins of hand-beaded buckskin, his straight muscular body decked out in feathered, fringed deerskin, his long hair braided with wild bird feathers, his eyebrows dyed black, his eyes painted in semicircles of red these gave him an aura of royalty. In one nostril, Micanopy wore a silver ring. Over his ears, he hung silver strands of beads, and circular pieces of silver covered his fitted tunic. All his wealth was on display.

John Hawk's poor collection of Spanish coins suddenly paled in comparison.

Black Dirt invited Luis, John Hawk, and Micanopy to his house. "We can have corn and coffee," he said. As he led them through the street in the heat of the day, John noticed that some of the homes were blackened by fire. St. Augustine had been bombarded and besieged and set afire many times. Black Dirt opened the gate in a fence that surrounded his home. His house had a sheltered porch like the chickees of the Seminoles.

Black Dirt took his guests to his cookhouse in the garden. Here, as they talked, he shucked some corn and put the yellow ears into water to boil. Then he invited the men into his living room, in the center of which was a metal-lined brazier, a heating unit in which coal would be placed to warm the room in winter.

Black Dirt said, "It's all we need. Few homes in St. Augustine have a fireplace."

As they ate the corn and drank hot coffee, Black Dirt said he wanted to go to the slave auction. He could not bid nor could he afford to buy a slave, he admitted.

They walked in the late afternoon to St. George Street and hovered at the edge of the crowd, waiting for the auction to begin.

When the bidding started, it was so fast John could hardly follow what happened. In horror mixed with fascination, John Hawk watched the bidding for a thick-set man who stared at the crowd defiantly with despising eyes. The slave was led away by a white man a full foot shorter than he.

"I feel sorry for the fellow," Luis muttered. "That master is Bulow. He has a reputation for cruelty."

"He so mean," Micanopy said, "I cheat him on purpose."

Now the bidding was for a lovely dark-skinned woman with shining hair to her shoulders, a woman who reminded John Hawk of his mother. The young woman trembled and cowered, wrapping a black shawl close around her body.

John knew that a black man's bid would not be recognized, or he would have bid every last Spanish coin in his deerskin pouch.

The auctioneer acknowledged Bulow's bid on the girl. Black Dirt said in an undertone, "That there Bulow he got three hundred slaves. He had a shootin' match. The slave keepin' track of Bulow's shots made a mistake. Bulow turned his gun on him, shot him dead!"

"What about the law? Can he do that?"

"Slave law exacts a fine for killin' a slave," Black Dirt replied. "Who gonna drag Bulow to court?"

The auctioneer cried, "I got sixty pounds for this fine girl. Who'll bid seventy?"

"Smith here! Sixty-five!"

"I got sixty-five, now seventy from Bulow! Seventy . . . seventy!!" sang the auctioneer, "Who'll give eighty?"

"Usdin here! Eighty!"

"I got eighty .. . . eighty, eighty! Who'll bid ninety?"

Black Dirt sighed with relief. "If Usdin get that girl, she gonna have a decent life."

"Bulow here! Ninety pounds!"

"That's too cheap for this good girl," snapped the auctioneer. Stepping to the young woman, he drew away the shawl in which she wrapped herself. She stood stark naked, her body shaking like a stalk of wheat in the wind.

John Hawk smothered the cry that came to his lips. Seething with anger, he realized his blackness made any protest a threat to his own life. He wanted to run from the crowd as a child runs from a beating — cowed, terrified. The auctioneer's gavel pounded hard as he cried, "Sold to Mr. Bulow!"

The slaveholder Bulow picked up the shawl and flung it at the girl. Trembling, she could hardly drape it to cover herself. Bulow led away the sobbing girl, holding one end of the shawl with a careless fist.

"Stop that snivelin'!" he commanded.

Luis muttered, "No heart, that Bulow."

For a moment John and Luis stood apart, unable to console each other. Black Dirt observed, "When Bulow's father died, this Bulow wrote a song for a slave to sing at the graveside: 'Old Bulow's dead, gone to Hell! Here lib Massa, doin' well!'"

Could a man compose a song like that at the death of his father? What kind of father had Old Bulow been to rear so mean a son? John Hawk examined his feelings about his own father. Could he sing a song at his father's death? Something cold gripped his heart, something prophetic.

Deeply troubled, John Hawk was ready to leave St. Augustine with its slave auctions, its Spanish aristocracy, its gossip and rumors.

The four friends walked along the beach, John a little behind the others, listening to the waves break against the shore. John Hawk checked his canoe to make sure it was still safe, and was relieved that it was. A crab with fearsome claws crawled on the dark gritty sand.

Black children played in the twilight, singing "Ring-around-a-rosy," and John was touched. He had not heard that song since he was a boy on his father's plantation. A little girl grasped his hand and invited him to join the game.

He joined hands with the children and danced in their circle, singing. Waves lashed the shore. The spirits of sea sirens seemed as tormented as his own soul. His mother was a slave; the girl sold at auction this day reminded him sharply of his mother's condition. He would be free, he promised himself. He would never be a slave again.

10

On a bright summer morning, the sky as clean as sweet milk, the sun the color of corn, Osceola whittled a pipe from a corncob. Moved to a special joy as he watched Morning Dew fix coontie, he felt something in his breast, a radiance, a glow, a sense of the heroic. The feeling was like aiming a musket at a fleet deer and with one shot bringing home meat for the people of his hammock.

The heat danced on the corn. For a brilliant moment, Osceola held his heart in a dream beneath earth and sky. He lay back and closed his eyes. The sun on his eyelids made the world orange, red, hot, beautiful.

Morning Dew had been only a small girl when Osceola had rescued her from Negro Fort. He was used to having her around. He had hardly noticed how lovely a woman she had become. His longing to embrace her caused him to move about restlessly, full of wonder at his new emotions.

He went to her side and said, "Morning Dew?" speaking her name just to hear himself say it.

"Osceola." She smiled. The summer rain last night had left the earth damp, smelling of sap and lemon blossoms. Birds flitted in the trees. A wild turkey gobbled at the edge of the clearing.

Osceola yearned to tell her something, but he had no words to express these deep emotions. Morning Dew seemed to bounce on her knees, a girlish act that made Osceola sure she was in a delirium of bliss at being noticed, at last. He did not need to say anything. He held out his hands, she took them, and he raised her to her feet.

A few days later, the Seminole marriage ceremony brought friends of bride and groom to the Cuscowilla hammock. Osceola had gone into the woods to be alone for a few days. Now he rode back into the hammock on Sam, the best horse in the Seminole village. Dismounting, he accepted the peace pipe from the circle of village fathers. He drew on it. Then the pipe was passed from hand to hand, exchanged between John Hawk and Osceola several times as a sign of friendship.

Osceola wore egret feathers in his turban, a brilliant cape, kilts, and strings of bright beads. John Hawk remembered the first time he had met Osceola. It was difficult to believe that this dignified chief, leader of the Seminoles, was that half-naked boy of a few years earlier.

He remembered how Osceola had encouraged him to run away, leave the plantation of his father forever. Osceola was like a brother, the only relative he really recognized.

Surrounded by Indian women, Morning Dew was lovely in a white doeskin dress with fringed hem and beaded waist, her cheeks bright with color and excitement, her almond-shaped eyes velvet soft and brimming with joy.

The ceremony began with Osceola taking from his belt a handful of colored sticks of unequal length. These he had prepared in the forest. Now he offered them to all the unmarried girls, who each coyly drew one. The bride knew which color she must select for the shortest stick, for it was an honor to receive the shortest stick when it meant volunteering for dangerous duty in war. Now the shortest stick won the groom. Naturally, she drew the red stick and waved it with a triumphant gesture above her head. The Indian women broke into shrieks of giggling.

John Hawk led his horse to the couple for the marriage trot around the village. Osceola lifted Morning Dew to the back of

Sam and jumped up behind her. He spurred the horse. The couple rode around and around, while the women nodded with pleasure and the men drank firewater and ignored the ceremony. When Osceola lifted Morning Dew from the back of Sam, the whole village gathered around a roasting deer. Baskets of food were set out for a feast.

Perhaps weddings are contagious. Within a month, a runner brought an invitation to Osceola for everyone in the village to attend the marriage of Wild Cat to Hummingbird. She, too, was a survivor of the massacre at Blount's Fort. John Hawk wanted to go to the wedding. So did Morning Dew, Osceola, his mother, and many others who had never been to Philip's village, a day's journey by horse.

John, eager to see if Chumpee was as attractive as he remembered her, set out on Sam. About twenty horses followed, in single or double file. John had come to cherish this horse above all his earthly possessions. He sat easy on the horse, riding with pleasure through the high pinelands, rich open savannas, undulating fertile hills where Indians dwelled in small, lush green hammocks. Now and then they met a group from other villages bound for the wedding.

Sam seemed to reciprocate John's affection. John felt comfortable and content on the journey.

For centuries, Seminoles lived in this hot, humid climate, with terrible swarms of insects. The Indians built open platform chickees that provided shade to catch the breeze. In one village after another, John and Osceola recognized friends who offered corn, vegetables, and grilled fish.

The Seminoles were acclimated to the intense heat, but United States troops coming to live in the forts fell ill.

When Andrew Jackson became the first governor of Florida, the worst fears of Indian leaders were realized as government troops poured into forts. King Philip invited the officers from the nearby fort to Wild Cat's wedding.

King Philip grasped each man by the elbows in turn, and

touched the forehead of each officer with a white feather attached to a stick. Then the men — red, white, and black — sat on the ground in a huge circle and passed the calumet, each taking a long puff.

The officers did not shed an inch of their formal wool uniforms, tightly buttoned to the collar, with long sleeves and heavy boots. Sweat poured from their faces. Though they tried to look detached from their discomforts, both from the heavy heat and not knowing exactly what was expected of them, many were pleased to have been invited.

What a story this would make when the officers were home in New York, New Jersey, or Massachusetts. Hesitant at first, the uniformed officers at length joined the war whooping, yielding to the hospitality of their Indian hosts. Soon the white man's imitation birdlike cries were added to the full-blooded Indian whooping and hollering.

John shook hands with a young officer about his own age, dark-eyed, dark-skinned. They could almost have been brothers, so alike were they.

"You don't look like an Indian," the young soldier said. He introduced himself as Francis James.

"You look awful hot," John said. "Why don't you take off your coat?"

Francis James quickly removed his gold-braided coat and hung it on the limb of a tree. He commented on the officers, who formed, he said, a "military aristocracy. They come from 'the best families.'"

He observed that the enlisted men, paid only six dollars a month, were a hard-bitten lot — drunks, fugitives, emigrants who could hardly speak English — but they suffered from the war as much as the officers did.

Years later, John Hawk learned that this young officer, who came from one of the "best families," had become so disgusted with the war against the Indians that he had gone home and put a bullet through his brain.

Now, in King Philip's village, an Indian drummer beat a syncopated rhythm, and the voices of the men joined the drummer's song, piercingly high and strong.

Though it was unusual for an Indian woman to speak the welcoming address, King Philip's wife had been taught white men's language and customs at a convent school, and she greeted all the guests. She prayed for peace.

Black Dirt sat erect, listening with a severe proud expression. John Hawk knew that Black Dirt had very little hope at all for peace between the Indians and the whites. Black Dirt believed that eventually there would not be an Indian alive in all Florida.

Luis Pacheco and his father wore suits of the latest fashion. Luis looked handsome in the white man's outfit.

Wild Cat's mother took her daughter's hands, and the two women led a slow dance, a dignified movement like wheat waving in the wind. Behind Chumpee and her mother came Osceola's mother and Morning Dew, and Redbird with King Philip's elderly mother. Strings of deer hooves seemed like bells at their ankles — ringing, sparkling, twinkling, like the sound stars might make. The women danced, their doeskin-fringed dresses swaying, their moccasined feet keeping time with the drums.

When the women's dance was done, the warriors, chanting to the rhythm of the drum, their ankles and legs decorated with turtle shell and coconut shell rattles filled with pebbles, sprang forward with great war whoops.

Blacks joined the dance that exploded with enormous energy. The shadows of the dancers leapt on the pounded dirt. In the clearing surrounded by ash and weeping willow trees, the dance went on and on, for hours. During the pauses, young Indians wrestled. Blacks, some of them slaves to Micanopy, made bets on the wrestling. If they won, Micanopy was obliged to give them their freedom. Whenever there was a winner, there was great celebration among the runaways.

With nightfall, the air cooled and the Indians lit huge bonfires. The shadows assumed giant shapes cast by the firelight flickering on dancers, trees, wrestlers, and celebrants. John Hawk, happy to be close to the lovely Chumpee and surrounded by friends, sprang from a squat into the midst of the dancers, whooping wildly. On his ankles, strings of deer hooves rattled. He whirled around and around, emitting low throaty notes, the dance possessing him. Hot sweat rolled down his forehead and cheeks and from his armpits. He felt exultant.

King Philip invited the white officers to join the dancing. With serious faces, and without removing their hot jackets, the officers tried to imitate the quick skipping, leaping motions, and hummed along with the Indians' songs. Though willing, the whites in their shining black boots seemed awkward. They stepped down hard, skipped, stomped, as sweat poured down their faces.

The Indians had not had such a good crop for many moons. The runaway blacks had come with knowledge of planting, and some had brought seeds from their masters' plantations. Now the older blacks and Indians, showing no sign of fatigue, danced and sang joyously. Soon the white officers begged off, exhausted. A few went so far as to remove their heavy wool blouses and to accept a drink of the Indians' firewater.

A gourd was passed from hand to hand. It was *assi*, a black, bitter-tasting drink. John Hawk detested *assi*, and only pretended to take a sip. Then he watched with quiet amusement the expression of the white officers who turned up the gourd and gulped. One man's eyes bugged out. He covered his mouth with his hand and gagged. Another soldier ran off into the forest to vomit.

Some Indians genuinely enjoyed assi. Each brave swallowed a mighty mouthful and then gave a war cry: "*Yohola!*" Osceola gave voice to this salute, for some said it was from this drink he got his name, *assi* and *yohola* from the war cry.

An officer introduced himself to John Hawk, "Wiley Thompson, the Indian agent."

John had heard of Thompson, and as they shook hands, John spoke his name with a sudden sense of poignant yearning, like a bell ringing in his mind. It seemed to John that of all those in the clearing at Wild Cat's wedding, John Hawk was the most rootless. Among Seminoles, he considered himself black. Among blacks, he thought of himself as an Indian. Among whites, he was regarded as mulatto. It was true that Luis Pacheco was also the son of a black woman and a white master, but Luis was loved by his father, and that made the big difference.

John Hawk glanced longingly at Chumpee. The smooth sweep of her black hair from a calm brow gave her face the appearance of purity and faith. For a moment she seemed unattainable, even foreign to him. She had had parents, friends, and family near her all her life. John Hawk believed himself alone among men, a loner.

Wait! he admonished himself. This was a celebration. Why had he become so serious? Couldn't he just enjoy the wedding? Why not have fun as everyone else did? He felt as if he had been carved of wood, the way Indians sometimes carved god-symbols.

John Hawk wondered: if this were his wedding, would he be so hospitable to the white men? Would he want Gen. Wiley Thompson at his wedding? Nearby was Negro Abraham, the man's black face a mask, like stone. John knew that Abraham had been born a slave and had fled from his master, a doctor. Abraham had become the slave and "sense bearer" to Micanopy. John Hawk admired Abraham's polished manners and his fine way of speaking English. Abraham had not joined the dancing. When Abraham sang, the low voice had a difference, a racial difference. If John Hawk closed his eyes, he could say which of the voices came from the throat of the black man, which from the white man, which from the Indian.

At last, the moon sank into the black beyond. The officers and chiefs separated, shaking hands and speaking words of peace. Nowhere was there a sign of a rifle or gun.

How curious John had been to see if Wild Cat's sister was as pretty as he remembered her. He found her breathtakingly beautiful. Her face gleamed like a lake in the moonlight, radiant, calm. He could not forget his first view of her as he had come into King Philip's village. Chumpee's face, steamy from the fire over which she had helped cook the wedding feast, still seemed like a perfect rose.

When she came and put her hands on John's arms, a warmth and sweetness came from her. John's head spun as if he had had too much firewater. Ah, he told himself, marriage must be like measles—contagious. First Osceola, now Wild Cat. Maybe John Hawk could escape the disease. To get an idea was one thing; to succumb was another. Still, if Chumpee would have him, if she would marry him, he might at last have a real family. A wife would give him a relative, one he had chosen himself, the best kind. Marriage might give him roots.

He walked with King Philip back to the family's chickee. He tried to think of the right words for a royal father. How could he ask King Philip if he might marry Chumpee? He, John Hawk, who was only a runaway. His courage failed him, and he said goodnight and shook hands. With head bowed, he walked away.

King Philip called after him, "If it's Chumpee you want, her mother and I are willing . . ."

11

Back in Cuscowilla, John Hawk was elected spokesman for the village, as white men came repeatedly to negotiate with the Indians for their land. White men now expected the Indians to abandon Florida. All this territory which had been the Seminole world for hunting, fishing, and growing food now was to become the property of white settlers.

Six months passed before he had a chance to go to King Philip's village again, this time to discuss with him the demands of the white man. Osceola and his wife and his mother traveled on horseback with John Hawk.

King Philip urged John to consider an early marriage with Chumpee.

Osceola and Morning Dew, Wild Cat and Hummingbird, John Hawk and Chumpee sat with King Philip and his wife late into the night. At dawn the next morning the three young couples went on horseback to watch the sun rise over the forest. Birds began to sing and twitter, welcoming the rosy dawn. A cock rendered a hornlike crow. Mists rose, and then the sun turned the sky a lovely pink and gold.

Chumpee leaned from her horse to slip her hand into John Hawk's. In the soft light of the sun, her smile was as trusting as a child's, encouraging him. She seemed to him the essence of innocence. A warmth and happiness flowed through him. Ahead Osceola and Morning Dew trotted their horses, and behind him Wild Cat and Hummingbird walked their horses. Surrounded by friends, John Hawk felt a great engulfing joy, and he began to laugh.

Chumpee, gazing at him shyly, laughed too. He slid off his horse and drew her from her horse, and they embraced.

In a week it would be Green Corn Day, on which marriage ceremonies were considered lucky.

The wedding of Chumpee and John Hawk was celebrated with the bride in white silk cloth that Luis Pacheco had brought from Fort King. She wore silver bells on her ankles. She clasped John Hawk about the neck as she had witnessed white women do at the fort with their husbands. John Hawk, embarrassed, chastened her with a soft chuckle. She whispered, "All is peace."

Chumpee offered John Hawk a cup of sparkling well water, and she sang the peace song of the Seminoles.

After the men had danced for hours, Chumpee began a foot-shuffling dance. Her friends joined her — Morning Dew and Hummingbird, Osceola's mother, and her own mother. The women swayed as they shuffled along, the fringes of their dresses blowing, their stepping slow and relaxed. The soft April sun glowed on them, full of promise. Already the heady perfume of orange buds filled the air. Some of the women wore sprigs of orange blossoms pinned in their black hair.

Never had John Hawk known such happiness. Indians with whom he had lived since coming to Florida as a boy gave him many gifts: pottery, handwoven straw baskets, blankets, an old knife newly sharpened, feathers, a chicken, a duck, a string of dried fish, a silver spoon, leather moccasins for himself and Chumpee, a warm sheepskin jacket.

When Green Corn Day faded to night, John Hawk and his wife ate by themselves at their own fire in King Philip's village. The firelight glowed on Chumpee's lovely tea-colored face and lit up her dark, almond-shaped eyes. Her hand rested in his. John Hawk felt at one with the earth and proud of his manhood.

Chumpee seemed a bird who had been caged and whom he had set free to soar, a beautiful strange seabird. This was not a realistic thought, for Chumpee had always had more freedom than John, having been born in an Indian village where children were cherished.

Her long, slender legs seemed as delicate as a bird's; her bosom soft, as feathers. She wore her long, shining black hair in a thick braid that fell against a pretty shoulder. John's eyes lingered on the back of her neck as she knelt by the fire to prepare supper. That lovely curve of the nape where the tender black hairs grew enticed him, and he kissed her there for the first time. She turned to him with ecstasy in her eyes, a faint flame in her cheeks.

John Hawk would always believe the best thing he ever did was marry Chumpee. She was calm and cheerful. When she cooked, she served the food as an offering of love. His heart melted to think of her. She was quiet and kept her conversation mostly for her women friends. She listened intently when he talked to her. It seemed to John her answers were well-considered and wise. She farmed with the other women in the fields and took care of the aged and the ill.

Life with Chumpee was good. But there was deep concern in the village. Micanopy had come several times to report that the white men wanted a treaty with the Seminoles, but so far no powwow had been arranged. The Seminoles had moved south years earlier to please the white man. They did not want to move again. The Seminoles liked their villages and had no desire to leave them.

12

Chumpee had not seen her brother Wild Cat for many years. When the call came for a powwow with the white man by the flowing banks of the Oklawaha River, Chumpee quietly urged John Hawk to go. John Hawk would be the Seminole spokesman. Chumpee, eager to see her husband in so important a role, hoped also that Wild Cat would bring Hummingbird and his daughter Little Sparrow.

Sam was almost dancing and prancing as the Cuscowilla delegates took off. Osceola, Morning Dew, and Chumpee led the way, and John Hawk followed on Sam.

Micanopy, King Philip, and Arpeika were already camping by the river when John Hawk arrived with the group from Cuscowilla. Micanopy had painted his face and chest and wore a silver ring in his nostrils. He was full of dire predictions about dealing with the white officers. Black Dirt had come from St. Augustine with Negro Abraham. Alligator and Charlie Emanthla had come from the Emanthlas' village.

Wild Cat arrived the next morning with Hummingbird and his daughter. He introduced Little Sparrow to John Hawk with the pride that most Indians reserve for sons only. Sparrow could outride and outrun any boy her age, Wild Cat boasted. In a white doeskin dress cut from her mother's wedding gown, the little girl rode a full-sized horse in a great circle around the camp. Everyone exclaimed over her ability to sit so well on a saddleless horse. She aimed her bow and arrow time after time toward a target, making repeated bull's-eyes. When the white men arrived and began to watch her skill, they broke into applause. The Indians sang a little song of praise: *Hoya, hoya, hoya, oooya* . . .

Wild Cat passed the peace pipe. In his bright-colored scarves that flowed in the wind and his feathered headdress, he looked every inch a chief.

"Now we will hear the treaty," John Hawk proposed.

Col. James Gadsden had served in the War of 1812. In 1818, serving Gen. Andrew Jackson, he had already fought the Seminoles. Gadsden thanked the Indians for coming.

"Some of you had to travel long distances. We're pleased you are here."

Then, seeing John Hawk's gaze on the treaty, Gadsden began to read it. As federal commissioner, he had been in charge of forcing Seminoles to move to south Florida in 1823.

John Hawk heard the Indians muttering, "No, no, never."

The usually placid Indians did not hide their agitation. The cries became loud, their objections plain: "No! No, never!"

Osceola interrupted, "This is our home. We moved once before. Why should we move again?"

Gadsden spoke evenly, "Please allow me to finish reading the treaty."

"No!" John Hawk stepped forward angrily. "There's nothing in this treaty to appeal to the Seminoles."

"But my mission is to have you hear this treaty read. We have worked hard to frame it," Gadsden insisted. He began to read again, pronouncing every legal-language syllable. His voice droned on and on. The Indians learned nothing more than they had understood from the first sentences. The government in Washington demanded that the Indians leave Florida.

Osceola, grim, speaking between his teeth, responded in a flat voice. "Let us have twenty years to consider. When twenty years have passed, we will discuss the treaty."

Colonel Gadsden gave him a cold hard stare. "Twenty years! That is just too many moons."

"We signed a treaty at Moultrie which still has eleven years to run," John Hawk reminded the colonel.

"Yes," added Micanopy, supporting John, "we did sign that treaty."

"Unless you sign," Gadsden replied angrily, "your funds from the government will be cut off."

Wild Cat was beside himself. "That was the money we were promised because we left certain lands and moved south. We took our families! We moved! We gave up good farm land, animals, orange groves, homes."

"You have no choice!" cried Colonel Gadsden, his face very red.

Micanopy drew aside the Seminole delegation, and they huddled, talking all at once — something rare for Indians. They were a people who prided themselves on speaking little, saying only what was essential. But being told that they had no choice had hit like a slap in the face. An ominous silence followed. The Indians wrapped pride about themselves like blankets. John Hawk, desperately trying to keep the Seminoles unified, had never seen Osceola so angry and upset. Micanopy's bull-dog face was grim, determined.

The white delegation and the Indians stood apart in silent challenge, waiting to see who would give in. Yet the Indians knew the great military might of the nation that opposed them.

Micanopy spoke quietly in Seminole with Black Dirt and Negro Abraham. Then he turned to John Hawk and uttered a few words in English to Gadsden, "The Seminoles are willing for seven chiefs to go west to inspect this territory to which you would send us."

A wary expression crossed Gadsden's face. With a nod, he acknowledged that anything was better than nothing. He agreed.

Negro Abraham said, "I speak Creek. I will go along as interpreter. We must sound out the Creeks. Ever since Creeks rounded up runaway slaves for return to Georgia slaveholders, Seminoles regard Creeks as sworn enemies."

"Creeks?" Gadsden was puzzled by all these Indian tribes and their inability to make peace amongst themselves. An Indian was an Indian, right?

The treaty was spread out on the stump of a tree. When the pen was proffered to Micanopy, he shook his head. Osceola, King Philip, and Arpeika bluntly refused to accept the pen. An ugly pause followed.

Since the Seminoles had moved south, the government had been providing funds for Indian survival. The Indians had come to depend on this money. They could not grow their own food in quantities to feed the tribes or hunt or gather fruit or berries on lands the white men now owned.

John Hawk thought there could be little harm in seven chiefs going west to inspect the land the government wanted to assign the Seminoles. He thought a trip at government expense to a part of the country he might otherwise never see could be an adventure. Sure, he would go. So would Alligator and Charlie Emanthla. All three stepped forward and signed the treaty.

Holata, Charlie's father, stepped forward and signed an X; Coa Hadjo, Jumper, and Black Dirt followed. Seven signatures.

John Hawk glanced over to the river's edge, where Chumpee and Hummingbird were talking in what seemed like an endless exchange. The morning was beautiful — a blue-white brilliant sky, wild daisies, buttercups, Indian paintbrush, poppies, and dandelions like a carpet of color. How could there be such tension in so lovely a world?

Gadsden trusted that he had a treaty. But the seven men who volunteered to go west believed they were going out to look at what would become Indian Territory and judge its suitability. The Indians did not want to buy a pig in a poke. Gadsden assured the Indians they would not be forced to move. The powwow ended without handshakes.

Charlie Emanthla and his father, Holata, insisted the Indians in Florida would be slaughtered like cattle if they refused to emigrate. Holata, Negro Abraham, and John Hawk had dealt with white men and all feared and distrusted them. John's memories of life on a slave plantation led him to agree with the Emanthlas. Eventually all the Indians would be forced out, one way or another, from the lush, lovely rain forests of Florida.

On Sunday, Luis Pacheco came to Cuscowilla, and when he heard that John Hawk was going west, he said, "I would love to go along."

John Hawk would have liked having Luis along. They were good friends. But the next best thing to having Luis was having Sam, his beloved horse. Between animal and man, there could be no more loving relationship than John had with Sam, he thought.

"That time we went to St. Augustine, that's the furthest I ever got from Pacheco's plantation," Luis observed.

Though his father was good to him, Luis was afraid to ask permission to go west with the seven chiefs. Luis expected to be free eventually. His emancipation was the most important thing in his life. His master had promised and had shortened the length of service Luis had agreed upon originally. Luis was rigidly careful not to offend a man who had made such a generous promise.

On a clear, rain-washed September morning in 1832, Chumpee saddled up Sam. "I think you love this horse more than you do me," she said with a twinkle in her eye. He felt a great tension at leaving her.

"Yes," he teased, "but I love you better than I do any dog on the plantation."

She filled a goatskin with clear water and wrapped a baked turkey, wild oranges, and berries in cabbage leaves. John wondered if he would ever see Chumpee again.

He mounted Sam and rode to the fork in the dirt road

where the six chiefs waited. An hour later they were joined by Maj. John Phagan, United States Army. The eight horses walked single-file. John Hawk felt confident on the back of his faithful Sam.

Excited with that anticipation which voyages often promote, John Hawk felt partly apprehensive, partly eager. Beneath him, the horse trotted lively.

Under a hot high sun, they kept up a steady pace, following the straight uniformed back of Major Phagan. Now and then they stopped to let the horses drink in a stream and they washed themselves or drank clean water and relieved themselves. The blankets, flung over the backs of the horses, were hot and scratchy, but by nightfall the chiefs were glad to have them to keep off the cold winds.

For eighteen hours they rode the wearying horses. At last they came to the West Coast of Florida overlooking the Gulf of Mexico. Major Phagan conferred with the captain of a ship which had been chosen for the crossing of the gulf. Leading their horses, the Indians climbed the gangplank and stood on the deck of the steamboat.

John Hawk leaned against the railing and watched the lights of Tampa Harbor receding. That night, he used his blanket for a bed on deck, remembering his first sea trip many years earlier when he was a runaway. John had been frightened then, but not so scared as the time he had fallen into quicksand, or the time he had been attacked by a shark . . . The gentle dipping of the steamboat lulled him to sleep. Rarely in his lifetime had he been so tired.

Awakened by a bright golden sun in his eyes, he momentarily had no idea where he was. The world is like that, incomprehensible and full of surprises. John roused himself and saw that the boat was near a wharf. New Orleans. He jumped off the boat and ran across reverberating splintery boards to the French Quarter. Fat black women there bought fresh fruit from sidewalk stands. John Hawk hungrily eyed red tomatoes, strawberries, and cucumbers piled up colorfully. The delicious odor of frying bacon and brewing coffee came to his nostrils. In a cafe where blacks were eating at long tables, he ordered thick shrimp creole gumbo, rice, and okra. He paid for it with government coins.

Optimistic, he marveled at the spicy, wonderful taste of gumbo and his sense of freedom. Walk into any cafe and buy prepared food! He could walk away and never be beholden again to any man. He could find work and send for Chumpee . . . and live in New Orleans.

Along the narrow bricked streets, dark-skinned women walked, their coffee-color like his own. The women were beautiful and appeared to him pampered with silks, pearls around their throats, hair piled up attractively, their feet in slim leather shoes. They seemed to John untouched by hardship or the knowledge of slavery. Their long, bright dresses brushed the wooden wharf. These women seemed respectable and genteel. Just a few years before, he had seen a slave girl sold at an auction; now he was observing dark-skinned women, almost prim, smiling, laughing, gesturing, talking, carrying beaded purses. Surely there had to be money or treasure in those purses.

When he returned to the steamboat, John was told by Micanopy that Major Phagan had gone ashore to visit relatives. The boat would not depart until the next day.

John Hawk went to the beach for a swim. The waves were high, the water invigorating and refreshing, and that great sense of buoyancy and joy that hit him in the early morning remained. He stood in the water, shoulder-deep, and shouted the words of an Indian war dance.

He dried himself, lying naked on the sand, then donned the trousers Chumpee had made, gathered up his few belongings, and went to see more of New Orleans. Red brick homes with ornate wrought iron balconies lined the streets. He peered through picket fences and open gates to courtyards where there were tall and leafy shaded gardens of tropical foliage, green and thick.

That night, beneath gas lamps, John Hawk loitered outside a theater while a glamorous crowd — women in soft garments, silks, wools, and velvets, with long white gloves, men in elegant shining top hats, silk coats, and slender polished shoes — opened for John a world he could not have imagined.

The next day the steamer departed. John had a basket of fresh strawberries from the market. He and Black Dirt compared adventures. Black Dirt, impressed by New Orleans, admitted he was reluctant to get back on the boat. "That was a mighty temptin' place to lay anchor."

The next stop was a bleak, uninviting town called Little Rock, where the chiefs left the boat to set out again on horseback in a cold, cutting wind. In hard rains and freezing snow, they made the final 200 miles across Arkansas into Indian Territory. There John Hawk met with the chiefs of Indian nations already settled — the Cherokees, Choctaws, Chickasaws, Kiowas, Comanches, and a few Seminoles. The hated Creeks were there too.

Here the tribes were only the last weak remnants of what had been noble Indian nations. In the shadow of the Ozarks lay a pleasant prairie between two branches of the Canadian River. The chiefs arrived in late October, winter accomplished, the wind blowing hard, the cold bitter. John Hawk rode Sam for many miles around Fort Gibson, and he saw nothing that would encourage him to move to this bleak land.

He stopped by a frozen stream and broke the ice for Sam to get a drink. The horse shivered as he swallowed the cold water. John Hawk put his arms around Sam and tenderly stroked the long, smooth neck. The horse ducked his head affectionately against John Hawk's shoulder.

Perhaps in spring or early fall this land might seem hospitable. Now the raw biting wind howled through bare branches standing bleak, black, barren against a gray threatening sky. At night, hailstorms rained chunks of ice as big as horse droppings. John had never seen hail. Hail this big could leave a monster lump on a man's head.

John, asked to sign a treaty that would bring to this prairie 7,000 Seminoles—all the Indians remaining in Florida, said no, he would not sign.

Holata and Charlie Emanthla signed at once. They said they saw the handwriting on the wall. Coa Hadjo, Jumper, and Black Dirt signed. Finally, hesitating, his conscience prodding him to continue to refuse, John Hawk took the pen in hand. Slowly, he signed his name. Negro Abraham, who had become the voice between two worlds, signed the treaty with an X. He wore an expression that puzzled John, for Negro Abraham seemed to be satisfied with himself.

For the first time, John Hawk was suspicious of Abraham, wondering if he might be in the pay of Major Phagan. He regarded Abraham with revulsion. Yet he himself had signed the treaty. Why did he expect greater resistance from Negro Abraham?

Abraham had the confidence of Black Dirt and Micanopy. He had once been Micanopy's slave and had won his freedom. John Hawk studied the stonelike black face and remembered the time he had seen Abraham eating with a white officer. Would Abraham betray his Indian friends?

In the stark military outpost of Fort Gibson, the seven Indian chiefs exasperated each other. They lived too closely, too intimately, too pressured. Now the winter cold kept the Indians from bathing in icy streams. They smelled terrible. Their clothes were dirty rags—torn, discarded army trousers. Their shoes were sandals made from broken saddles. In sharp contrast, the officers of the army wore starched white shirts and clean black coats and pants pressed by their women.

The white men bathed, shaved, and came from a hearty breakfast served by hired Indians. The Seminole chiefs often went without breakfast, or were served whatever was left over by the soldiers. John's mouth felt fur-lined. He was hungry.

Now the treaty was signed. What difference did it make?

Cakes and coffee were served, and everyone ate and drank. The officers had their second breakfast and were in a good mood now that the signing was done with. They were in a hurry to have the Indians return to Florida.

John Hawk dreaded the return trip. Suspicious of Negro Abraham, he kept a wary eye on the old man. Was Abraham a SPY? John Hawk hoped not, because he would hesitate to turn him over to the Seminoles, who knew how to treat traitors. Justice would be swift and harsh.

John stared at the treaty lying on the plain, pine table. He longed to snatch it up and tear it to shreds. He wished he had not signed it. The other Indians might claim they had not fully understood the terms of the treaty, but John Hawk could read and had no such excuse.

Within a few hours of the signing, the Seminole delegations went out into the wind and cold.

Where were their horses?

The Seminoles, accustomed to running great distances, searched in all directions. Their horses were nowhere to be found.

Finally, Major Phagan confessed that their horses, along with some belonging to the military, had been stolen by Pawnee raiders. With no other animals available, the seven Seminole chiefs would have to carry their provisions and packs on their backs and walk back to New Orleans.

John Hawk, his grief as open as the sky, set out on the long walk with tears streaming down his face. Sam was gone. Sam, his faithful horse, the gift of King Philip; Sam, his best-loved beast who had carried him so many thousands of miles. Sam was gone.

13

On the walk back to Cuscowilla, John Hawk and Black Dirt exchanged intimate confidences and became good friends. Familiar with the route because his Uncle Osuchee had been chief of the Lake Ahpopka tribe living in this area, Black Dirt followed the river much of the way.

Coil on coil, the dark brown water of the Chattahoochee River slithered within its flower-decked banks. Under a golden sun, frogs complained and croaked. Olive-green silt rose to speckle the surface of the river with rainbow hues.

Black Dirt spoke of his Uncle Osuchee's distress at the new roads carved out of the jungle by the white man.

"My Uncle Osuchee was the blackest black man I ever knowed."

John Hawk had to smile, for Black Dirt was the blackest, jet black man he knew.

"How did you get that name?" asked John.

Black Dirt laughed humorlessly. "I picked it myself. People think black's got a bad meaning. Like 'That was a black day in history.' Or a 'black lie.' But in our village when I was little, each person could have a piece of earth to plant. He could eat what he growed or sell it. You should have seen them plots, how they got tended. Sometimes we growed flowers. Squaws growed beans, peas, corn, yams cucumbers, watermelons. When I tells my mother I need a plot of my own, we goes lookin' and she knelt and put her hand in the soil. She say, 'This be good black dirt.'

"Good black dirt. From that dirt comes nourishment for life itself. That summer," Black Dirt continued, "I became a man. I puts in seed, I pulls weeds, I watched the garden grow. In black dirt. Man, that's life!"

Black Dirt was becoming now what he had always been becoming—a man. And considering that fact, John Hawk realized he too had become what his name meant him to become—a Hawk, a Seminole.

"Black is good. Or bad. A color has no special meaning. Only the meaning we give it," Black Dirt continued. "We say a big yellow sun. The sun can warm you or burn you up. That don't make yellow good or bad. When I was a kid, I wonder why a brave looked for a light-skin girl to marry. An ugly light-skin girl be married before a pretty girl with black skin. It do worry me. I was only a little kid when I picked my name and got rid of my baby name."

In a sheltered spot, in the darkness, they lay down to sleep, covering themselves with leaves and soft brush. At daybreak, refreshed, John Hawk and Black Dirt bathed in the river and set out for Cuscowilla. Black Dirt lived in St. Augustine, but he was familiar with towns. "I avoids town in summer. They gets fever epidemics."

John Hawk and Black Dirt approached the hammock that seemed so green and lush, sparkling in the midmorning sun. The Indians' platforms on stilts and the thatched roofs welcomed the footsore chiefs. John stopped at the roofed-over well to drink the clear water. Bordering the sedgy lagoon in the dense cypress forest were cabbage palms and pine trees. A dog barked in recognition of John Hawk, and wagged his tail and jumped joyously around him.

Chumpee greeted him more quietly. "You are returned. *Hum-bux-chay!* Come eat!" She gently drew him toward their chickee.

Chumpee told him that the seven chiefs had been summoned to Gen. Wiley Thompson's headquarters. Thompson had been sent, she said, to replace John Phagan. Rarely in history had a man received retribution for cruelty as quickly as had John Phagan. At Fort Gibson, Phagan's accounts had been audited and found wanting. He had been pocketing government funds and was dismissed in disgrace.

Among the chiefs that Thompson asked to come see him were Micanopy, Abraham, Osceola, Jumper, Black Dirt, and John Hawk. The chiefs would go to the meeting. But they were already talking about making war rather than leaving Florida.

Thompson shook hands with each of the chiefs, repeated each name, and seemed surprised that the three black men Abraham, John Hawk, and Black Dirt — should be Seminole chiefs. "How do you want your stock and goods moved to Indian Territory?" he asked.

The chiefs were dumbfounded that Thompson would come so bluntly to his point. A look of desolation that comes with loss of dignity crossed Micanopy's face. He said, "If we move to the lands of the west, this is the end of the Seminole people."

Black Dirt said, "We fear that our Negroes will be seized on the move west and we'll be slaves again."

John Hawk glanced at the flat angry faces of his comrades. He studied Thompson's face and felt as if he could read the general's mind. "Damn their ugly hides," the general must be thinking. "How can I get it across to them they must leave? They have no choice."

"Micanopy," Thompson said, "you are an old man. Do this service for your people. Tell them to move west."

Micanopy resented the implication that his age should make him a traitor. He was no longer the strong slaveholder and influential chief he had once been. He was a despondent Indian who had walked a thousand miles through snow, sleet, and freezing cold. He now had arthritis and a nervous tic in his right eye. The squint gave him a sinister appearance. But he was not old. He was short and ate constantly since returning from the trip west. He now weighed 300 pounds, and waddled like a duck when he walked.

John Hawk spoke up. "We went out to inspect Indian Territory with the understanding that if the land did not find favor in our eyes, we would not be forced to move. We did not like the land. We do not want to live among Creeks. The Creeks accepted bribes and rewards from the United States government for blacks taken from Seminoles. Our lives would be in danger in the West. The Creeks are slave catchers."

Thompson put a heavy finger on the signed treaty on his desk. "John Hawk, you signed this treaty!" He pointed to John's signature, not an X, but a carefully written signature. Then he raised an angry finger and shook it at the others, "You! You! You put your marks on this treaty!" Furiously, he slammed his palm down on the treaty.

"Those marks don't mean we want to leave our homes," Jumper protested.

"No, we will not go," Black Dirt insisted.

Thompson's face was purple. "You will have a strip of land separate from the Creeks," he assured them.

John Hawk said, "We do not accept your words. The Creeks are rogues. We hate them. We cannot go to a land where snow covers the ground. Hail falls, big as a man's fist. We like it here. Here the sun shines, we fish in the ocean and rivers. If our tongues say yes, our hearts say no. Our horses were stolen by the Pawnee. We walked a thousand miles."

Black Dirt added, "We thought your officers would be satisfied if we set down our X. Leave us this last little part of our land here."

In a mirror behind Thompson, John Hawk saw his reflection. Indians kept no mirrors, and John Hawk rarely saw himself in a glass. He was a tall, broad-shouldered man with curly black hair, coffee-colored skin, glowing good health, big black flashing eyes. His was not the look of a coward. Behind him he could see reflected in the mirror a window looking out on an area around the Agency Office where Indian children played, women carried bundles, and Seminoles held rifles and hunting supplies.

Thompson spoke, "You have no choice. I am an honest Christian, an officer and a gentleman. I wish I knew how to explain to you that time is running out. The government pays me a salary to move you Indians to the West. You have no choice," he repeated.

John Hawk replied, "The sentiments of the Seminoles have been expressed. We will not go willingly."

Osceola and the other chiefs nodded. Abraham spoke in the Seminole tongue to Micanopy. The Indian said, "We are resolved to remain here."

"General Thompson," said Osceola, "any chief who agrees to move west will be punished. I began life in Creek country in Alabama. My mother married a white man named Powell. My great-grandfather was Scottish, James McQueen. In the Battle of Tohopeka, a whole Indian community was slaughtered by Andrew Jackson's troops. It was not war. It was murder. My mother and an uncle, Peter McQueen, were the only survivors of my family. My mother took my hand and we walked with Peter to a Red Stick village. White men drove me from Alabama. Now they wish to drive me from Florida."

Thompson started to interrupt, but Osceola continued, "No! Listen! At the treaty of Moultrie, we were promised we could stay in peace on this land for twenty years. We were told that if we died, it would not be by the hand of white men but by nature. The fruit of bad neighbors is blood. The Seminoles stay!"

John Hawk felt proud of Osceola, of what he had said and the way he had said it. The chiefs turned to go in a grim single file.

John Hawk, Black Dirt, Osceola, and Jumper walked back to the hammock. The moon cradled a quarter moon in its arms. The sky, studded with stars, seemed low. As John Hawk approached his chickee, he could see his wife kneeling on the platform and hear her singing a tune that Indian children sing. He was glad to be home.

The next morning Luis Pacheco came with a St. Augustine newspaper. Chumpee prepared cornmeal for their breakfast. Luis showed John an advertisement that reported Thompson had $7,000 from the United States government to pay Indian claims. The last annuity would be paid on October 21, 1834. Claims had to be made to Thompson before that date, for the Seminole Agency would be phased out in Florida and all the Indians would be removed to the West.

Luis said, "All the newspapers report that President Jackson might give permission for the government to buy blacks from Indians. If we have a bad crop, starving Indians might even sell their friends."

Negro Abraham jumped up on the platform and Chumpee brought him a bowl of cornmeal mush. When John had first met Negro Abraham, John was drawn to the tall, courtly man called the "sense bearer" of King Micanopy. John liked talking to Abraham, because he had been told that Negro Abraham was able to read minds and the idea intrigued him.

Abraham was the first black man ever to speak to John about Africa. Negro Abraham had come on a slave ship when he was a child from a land of intelligent men, the Ibo people. Abraham had told John that among the Seminoles were many runaways who descended from the fighting tribes of Africa: Ibo, Egba, Senegalese, and Ashanti. Abraham had been taught English by a London woman and had picked up an English accent he never lost. He could behave like a prince of England; he had courtly manners.

Negro Abraham said in an accent like an Englishman's, "There will be a war between the Seminoles and the American army."

John Hawk recalled the unequal battle at Blount's Fort. His wife's eyes were wide with terror.

"Whites are greedy for this land," Negro Abraham said.

Luis advised the Indians to go to Thompson and collect whatever money he would give them.

"The white man never deals fairly with the Seminoles," Negro Abraham insisted. "He is cruel to blacks. We have to judge our paths, which way to go."

Luis read an editorial about Maj. John Phagan being dismissed from the army for mishandling funds. John Hawk laughed. He could recall John Phagan standing in the doorway of a fort on a bitter winter day, casually informing the Indians their horses had been stolen and they would have to walk back to Cuscowilla.

Luis said, "How many horses have you here?"

"Why?" John wondered.

"I hear American troops and Creeks are threatening to attack Black Dirt's uncle's village on Lake Ahpopka."

"We haven't a horse here. Not a single nag," John admitted.

"How about arms?" Luis asked.

"Arms, yes. Ammunition, guns, rifles . . . we got some from Thompson."

"Look," Luis said, "I know a stable near St. Augustine — plenty of horses."

"Whose plantation?"

"Bulow's!"

"I remember that rat who bought the slave girl at auction."

John was uncomfortable with the idea of a horse raid so close to St. Augustine. The whites were already looking for an excuse to shoot blacks on sight.

"If we're going to head off troops at Ahpopka, we gotta have horses," Luis argued.

John rested a reassuring hand on Chumpee. "Don't worry. Luis is experienced at such raids."

She did not reply, but John knew she was frantic with worry.

That February, in St. Augustine, the temperature dropped to seven degrees, and all of Florida was hit by a severe cold wave. Wild oranges and berries froze on the trees. The frozen streams made fishing impossible. The freeze drove bears and other game into hiding. The Seminoles returned from hunting with a rare half-starved rabbit or a tiny scrawny doe that could not feed a family, let alone a tribe.

John Hawk, pulling on the deerskin trousers and jacket Chumpee had created so well with needle and furs, gave his wife's braid a gentle pull and affectionately nuzzled her neck. He took up rifle and his father's ax and joined Luis.

At the edge of the sedgy swamp, Luis had two horses waiting; neither was saddled, but Luis flung old blankets over their backs to protect them from the bitter cold. Both men mounted easily and the horses trotted off.

Before the sun rose, John and Luis were joined by Jumper, Alligator, and Black Dirt. The men on stolen horses took the white man's new roads to the outskirts of St. Augustine. Luis was familiar with the large fence that surrounded Bulow's property and with the barn, because he had been there on Pacheco's business frequently. He had once bought two horses from Bulow.

In the dark of a moonless freezing night, Black Dirt loosened several planks of the fence. Working quietly and cautiously, John Hawk pried off a loosened plank. The noise of the board ripping from the fence seemed like an explosion. In spite of the cold, John's hands were sweaty. The Indians' horses were tied to a tree close to the fence. Two men slipped inside the barn. The animals, alerted to a strange presence, became restless and stamped their feet. John Hawk shivered with the cold and fear.

A second plank gave way to John's ax, making a space large enough to lead a horse through. Impatiently, Black Dirt pried at the bottom of a wide door of the barn, lifting it from the ground just enough to wiggle in on his stomach. Inside, he removed the pole that held the door closed. The door swung up with a resounding crack that frightened the animals. Nervous whinnies came from the horses.

"God!" Alligator whispered, "You'll wake the world!"

Alligator followed Black Dirt, and John and Luis raced after them into the barn. In pitch darkness, Luis grabbed John's wrist and led him through a huge hay-smelling area where at last his eyes became accustomed to the dark and he could see outlines of dozens of horses, restlessly aware of strangers in the barn. Black Dirt, already mounted, galloped the first horse out of the barn and through the narrow opening in the fence. Alligator rode one horse and led another by a leather leash. All of Bulow's horses seemed ready to run with the Seminoles, as the animals pawed the dusty earth.

John Hawk leapt on the back of a neighing, prancing horse. The smell of the animal was familiar, an odor John loved. Two more horses, neighing hysterically, galloped through the door and between the narrow planks of the fence, their whinnies almost human. John Hawk and Luis, on horses, each leading another horse by a hemp rope, raced through the opening in the fence and down the road. Black Dirt, in the lead, had all the original horses with which they had arrived in St. Augustine. A great burst of gunfire told the raiders, riding low, they had been discovered.

John Hawk could hardly suppress a cry of triumph. If he had to die, he wanted to die this way, in a heart-lifting adventure. None of the fear he had known as a boy, at the time he sank in the muck of quicksand or swam furiously from a threatening shark, touched him now. He felt above fear, suddenly, exhilarated rather than frightened. He told himself he had known the best of life—Chumpee, his honey-girl, his friends Osceola, Wild Cat, and Black Dirt. And now this great moment of success, riding a horse that felt familiar beneath him, and leading a filly on a rope. He sensed that he had recaptured one of his own stolen horses. That was divine justice, better than what had happened to John Phagan. John Hawk had come to believe in divine justice. With firing all about them now, John knew he was in danger. Yet he was confident no bullet would hit him.

He held his ax against his chest. A bullet whizzed dangerously close. With his friends, he urged the horses to a fast gallop. The pursuit into the woods lasted about ten minutes. Then the pursuers gave up, probably out of fear of getting too far from St. Augustine. Perhaps they were afraid of being caught by the Indians who were known to hide in trees and jump their enemies.

The sun rose on a cold day, the sky almost white. The men lay low, hiding in the marshy jungle, waiting for night. Black Dirt knew the best route to Lake Ahpopka. The men had gone to St. Augustine on five horses and were returning with fourteen.

When the sun had set again, Black Dirt led the riders with their captured horses on the new roads carved out of the woods by the white man. The starless night was pitch dark, the moon like ice. The horses seemed comfortable in the frozen forest. Black Dirt intuitively found the right roads. If starving Indians thought of selling their black friends for food, John thought, there would certainly be war, for the blacks would fight to death for freedom. He trusted the Indians as much as he did his black brothers. He felt closer to Osceola than to any other man on earth.

In the soft light of the following morning, near a half-frozen stream, they stopped to water the horses. Something vaguely familiar about the horse that Alligator led by the leather leash caused John to study the animal. Suddenly, the horse lifted its head and neighed in a low, gentle, knowledgeable way — a whinny that touched John's heart. He advanced with recognition and joy. The horse put his head down on John's shoulder and John embraced the long, smooth neck. It was Sam. The coincidence was almost too much to bear.

"Sam! Sam! I didn't think I would ever see you again!" John cried.

The horse whinnied as if trying to speak of its pleasure at being reunited with an old friend.

"Sam! Oh, Sam!"

14

Now that the Indians had horses, John Hawk believed he could deal with Wiley Thompson from a position of strength. He went to see Thompson to suggest another pow-wow. Thompson studied his calendar and suggested March 27 at Fort King because Gen. Duncan Clinch was coming. A soldier brought two cups of coffee. John sat opposite Thompson and enjoyed his first cup of good black coffee in months.

Thompson said, "General Duncan Clinch is a good man, John Hawk. I hope you will like him."

John Hawk wore the blank look he had learned from the Indians. He wondered if he could trust Thompson. And General Clinch? Even the name sounded threatening.

"Clinch is religious, and kind to his slaves," Thompson said.

John Hawk said nothing. Could a man who held another man in bondage be truly religious? Religion had more to do with what happened between man and man than what happened between man and God, he thought.

"I know you're worried about blacks being taken as slaves if you go west. If you agree to emigrate, you will all be emancipated. You can have a village of your own. Where is your rifle?" Thompson asked.

John Hawk flushed. He had lost it in the horse raid. Turning to a shelf behind him, Thompson reached for a rifle. "This is the latest model. It's a gift!"

Was it a gift or a bribe? An Indian did not refuse a present. That would be an insult. He thanked Thompson, and he left with the rifle. Jumping on Sam, he wondered: Did I walk into a trap?

At the end of March, 150 Seminoles, warriors and chiefs, gathered at Fort King. To deter snakes, a platform had been built on piles ten feet above the ground. Reptiles and vicious biting insects often made a forage into the soldiers' beds and clothing. Long ago the Indians had learned to build chickees above the ground and to wear loose clothing which protected them from insects and reptiles.

When John Hawk arrived with Cudjo, the garrison was drilling on the platform. An order was given for the soldiers to bring up rows of benches to be set on opposite sides of the platform—the Indians to sit on one side, the blacks on the other. John now identified so closely with Indians, he did not want to be separated from them. His lovely wife was a full-blood Seminole, daughter of an Indian chief.

That there were two separated rows of benches, one for former slaves and one for Indians, seemed a bad omen to John Hawk. Cudjo was the formal interpreter. Nicknamed King Cudjo, he held himself majestically, though he had suffered a paralyzing disease as a boy. He was among the chiefs who had walked back from the western country, even with his bad limp. Now he lived in Fort King and had a salary from the government. In the jargon of plantation slaves, Cudjo told John Hawk for the tenth time, "I's a runaway slave."

John Hawk replied, "Me too. Quit braggin'. The shame is on those who don't run away."

Cudjo had a reputation among the Seminoles of siding with the whites; he was "a good Negro." Cudjo had been useful to the whites and might be again. When the Seminoles were finally forced to go west late in 1837, Cudjo, despite his many favors to the white soldiers, was required to go with the refugees.

General Thompson stepped with authority up the laddered steps to the platform and stood behind a pine table. "I want you to know of my sympathy for the Seminoles and my genuine desire to help you." Then he read a letter he had written to the secretary of war.

"The Seminoles," he read, "own many Negroes who dread the idea of being transferred from their comfort and liberty to bondage and hard labor under overseers on sugar and cotton plantations. These former slaves have a great influence over the Indians. They live in villages separate, and in many cases, remote from their Seminole owners. They enjoy equal liberty with their owners, with the single exception that the slave supplies his owner annually, from the product of his little field, with ten bushels of corn. Everything else belongs to the slave. Some slaves have horses, cows, and hogs with which the Seminoles do not meddle. An Indian would almost as soon sell his child as his slave . . . The affection of the Indian for his slave, and the slave's fear of being sent back to the plantations, have caused the slaves to influence the Indians to resist departure from Florida."

John Hawk believed Wiley Thompson meant well. How could the general realize how offensive the term "slaves" had to be for a man who had been born in slavery and was now free? The blacks stirred restlessly, some growling in dismay. Among the white men there was polite applause. Then General Thompson read a letter from Andrew Jackson admonishing the Seminoles for breaking their word about departing for Indian Territory. Jackson insisted that the Indians had to migrate as they had promised.

General Thompson shaded his eyes against the blazing sun. "My children, you have no choice. You must go!"

Jumper rose. "We come to make talk today. We are all made by the same Great Father. We are alike his children. In the freezing winter, we are all cold. In the summer, we are all hot. Therefore, we are brothers. Let us not quarrel, and let us not allow our blood to rise one against another."

His words were more invocation than argument. General Thompson turned to John Hawk, as if to remind him of their talk and the gift of the rifle.

John Hawk rose. He had rehearsed a brief statement. "Let reason prevail." He choked up and could speak no more.

General Thompson introduced Gen. Duncan Clinch, "a pros-
perous planter from Georgia and Mobile, Alabama." Gray,
hugely fat, he weighed as much as Micanopy, in the neighbor-
hood of 250 pounds. John Hawk thought Clinch and
Micanopy balanced each other out on the platform.

General Clinch rose with obvious effort, his expression a
combination of disdain and pity. No doubt, a slaveowner like
General Clinch could not understand Indians willing to welcome and even marry runaway slaves. Clinch, probably used to
his own slaves who might have been childish, submissive,
even beastlike, might not understand blacks who were so ar-
ticulate and independent, behaving like braves.

General Clinch spoke: "I hope you will ratify the new treaty
quickly, for your sake as much as mine. You have no choice.
And I have a personal grief. I need to be home. I had a message that my wife died and left my eight children with no one
to care for them. If you refuse to go west, there may be a war.
And in a war, the U.S. Army will win."

Osceola leapt up, shouting angrily, "We are not children who
fear war. We have buried the hatchet, but we can unearth it!"

General Thompson cried, "But you all signed the Treaty of
Payne's Landing!"

Micanopy tried to get to his feet, then spoke from the
bench, "No, I say no." His voice was passionate as he repeated,
"No!" He began to speak in Seminole with vigorous gestures.

Thompson demanded, "What did he say, Cudjo?"

Cudjo had earned his name for reckless courage. He replied,
"He say we no go. We like this land well. We born here. He
not like to leave in old age. He say when last war hatchet was
buried, you promise no more trouble to Indians. He say he did
not sign at Payne's Landing, but now under President Jackson,
he say, 'Dig up hatchet.' He say he fear not death. He be ready.
It be duty for Indian tribes to die."

In a rage, Thompson angrily approached Micanopy with
the treaty and pointed to Micanopy's X on the paper. The

moon-fat face of the chief remained impassive.

Micanopy again spoke in Seminole. Cudjo translated. "Micanopy say he put his hand toward pen but not touch it. He no made X."

John Hawk clearly remembered the old man making his X. John suffered because he also knew he had signed his name legibly. It was a noose about his neck now.

"No more annuities, ever!" Thompson declared, striking the table. "Starve!"

Osceola, clearly contemptuous, replied, "The warriors of the Seminole nation do not require a penny from the Great White Father." Osceola continued, "I will kill with my own hands any chief who makes the first move from this land."

The effect of the promise was explosive. John Hawk said, "Allow us thirty days to consider the president's directive."

The well-spoken words of John Hawk calmed the hour. Thompson and Clinch consulted. Micanopy conferred with Cudjo and they left the platform. Clinch looked miserable, knowing that a council without the principal chiefs was of little use.

Holata Emanthla stood up. "My son Charlie Emanthla, and I, Holata, will sign the treaty. Black Dirt too. We have no choice. We are prepared to migrate."

Three chiefs out of 150 Seminoles. General Clinch appealed to the good sense of the Seminoles. "You will not be forced to live with Creeks. You will receive seeds, tools, blankets, and money. We will send horses and cattle with you. You may take seedlings of trees and whatever you wish from the land. But if you persist in remaining in Florida, there will be war."

Three chiefs came forward to sign: Holata Emanthla, Charlie Emanthla, and Black Dirt. Osceola, with a fierce expression, shot up like a deer. Instantly, every eye was on him. Before anyone could guess what was happening, a knife flashed through the air. Soldiers gasped. General Clinch turned pale. Osceola drove the knife through the paper on the table.

"This is my signature to any treaty with the whites!"

15

Thompson shouted, "Handcuff him! Lock him up!"

Soldiers surrounded Osceola and tied his hands behind his back with hemp rope. Indians and blacks rushed to Osceola's defense, and soldiers cocked their weapons. Osceola, sweat running down his face, fire in his eyes, showed defiance in every muscle.

Suddenly, with a huge earth-shattering crack, wood split, and the platform collapsed. Agents, officers, blacks, and Indians rolled and fell on each other. A great clamor of snapping stakes and the screams and cries of injured men rent the air. Cut and bruised by broken splintered boards, the men, buried together, struggled to rise or crawl out. Gunfire signaled the Fort that soldiers were endangered.

John Hawk pulled his leg from under a crushing stake. Blood rushed down his thigh and from his ankle. He exerted all his strength to rise. He was really all right, just bruised, but he could not seem to lift himself. Startled officers, their dignity gone, tried to get to their feet and out from under struggling, crying blacks and Indians. John Hawk realized he was on top of a white soldier, and he laughed. "For once in my life, I been atop a white man."

Thompson repeated his order: "Lock up Osceola! Get the Fort doctor to treat these injured men!"

Obviously, the powwow was over. While injured men pulled themselves, dazed and bloody, from the broken timbers, soldiers hustled Osceola toward the Fort prison.

John Hawk, finally out on the grass, faced General Thompson. Swallowing his pride, he selected his words with an array of false beginnings, "Please, General, sir, we have been friends. We trust each other. Please, sir, release Osceola in my charge."

Thompson hesitated and said, "Bring Osceola's wife to me at the Trading Post tomorrow."

Osceola would have to spend the night in jail. John's heart was heavy as he jumped on Sam to set out for Cuscowilla. Passing soldiers at target practice, John Hawk, who had long hunted with Indians, observed how superior the Seminoles were with arms. Some Seminoles watched target practice. The Indians looked scornful. Negro Abraham burst into loud laughter when an inept soldier shot off several rounds of ammunition without once hitting the target. The Indians shouted Seminole insults at the soldiers.

The sun was setting when John Hawk rode Sam to the edge of the clearing near Cuscowilla. Chumpee was waiting for him, and John Hawk dismounted and lifted Chumpee to Sam's back. The horse trotted back to the chickee, and John stretched his legs, running beside Sam. Chumpee had prepared a vegetable stew, and they sat down together close to the banked fire to eat.

"Osceola has been thrown into the white man's prison. I promised to bring back Morning Dew to the Fort."

Chumpee offered to go with Morning Dew. She needed sugar and coffee from the Trading Post. She had no food left in the chickee.

Both Chumpee and Morning Dew dressed in their best doeskin dresses with fringed hems and beaded waists. The long struggle against the soldiers had reduced the Seminoles to rags. Women now tore old clothes into strips and made long skirts of

105

patchwork stripes. Both Chumpee and Morning Dew wore these skirts most of the time. But for the trip to the Fort, especially with the mission of getting Osceola out of prison, they dressed carefully and wove egret feathers into their black hair.

Morning Dew, the daughter of an Indian chief and a black mother, was darker than Chumpee. According to slaveholding law, a child followed the condition of the mother. All blacks were slaves, so Morning Dew, in the eyes of the whites, was a slave.

General Thompson greeted John Hawk politely and bowed to acknowledge the introduction of Chumpee and Morning Dew. He suggested the two women go fetch their supplies, while he and John Hawk talked. As soon as the women left the room, Thompson said, "Your women are pretty."

Ordinarily, the remark might have melted John Hawk's icy mood, but he was hungry and concerned about Osceola. The children of Cuscowilla were starving.

Coffee was brought, and John Hawk stirred sugar into his cup. If Thompson divided and separated the Seminoles, how would John Hawk get Osceola released?

Suddenly, John's thought was cut sharply by a woman's terrified scream. John Hawk froze. He recognized that voice! Cudjo rushed into the office shouting, "Morning Dew! Slave catchers carried off Morning Dew!"

General Thompson did not move a muscle. John Hawk had the shocking sensation of finding the dregs of himself, odds and ends of evaporated identity, turned to ice. He could hardly speak, but forced the words, "What about Chumpee?"

Cudjo shook his head. "She's outside."

John Hawk stood up and shook his finger at General Thompson threateningly. If he had brought a gun, he could have shot the general. Silently, he swore vengeance on this man. From now on, General Thompson was his enemy. "You get back Osceola's woman or you're a dead man!"

"Don't threaten me!" General Thompson replied furiously. Although he seemed ready to run out of the office, he straightened his shoulders and walked to the door of the agency, crying, "Put this man in irons."

Cudjo stepped in front of John Hawk, as if to protect him. Indian braves, narrow-eyed, drew back against the walls of the fort in horror at the sight of John Hawk being surrounded by armed men and half-marched, half-dragged across the yard to the guardhouse. Indians, blacks, and soldiers stared in dismay at the victim, his bare legs still scarred and bloodied from the previous day's collapse of the platform.

John, wild and helplessly outnumbered, cursed himself for having fallen into the trap of bringing Morning Dew to the fort. He experienced a soul-rending savage anguish at the loss of his freedom. Thrown into a dungeon, slapped into irons, John Hawk felt his wrists and ankles locked in chains. A mug of water and dry bread was left near him. His heart pounded so hard he thought his chest would break open. His mind seemed to be splintering like shattered glass.

"Let me out of here!" he screamed.

"Take it easy," a voice warned.

Friend or foe? "Who's there?" he asked.

"Who do you think? Did you get yourself arrested to get me out?"

John Hawk, horrified in the darkness, unable to see his own feet, realized that he was near Osceola. John Hawk had not been a hero. He had been tricked. Now he had to tell Osceola that his wife was kidnapped. Calming himself, John was ashamed of wasting energy screaming. His cunning and reason reasserted, he realized he had not been so canny to get arrested deliberately. But now that he was with Osceola, they must think of a plan of escape.

"How long have I been in here?" Osceola demanded.

"About twenty hours."

"Seems like twenty months. What's going on?"

"Morning Dew's been kidnapped." John Hawk had managed to say it. Nothing in his life had required more courage.

Osceola moaned. Then, as if they were squatting by a fire with food and drink between them, they discussed plans to get out of the dungeon. Their first task was to retain energy and not get depressed. How could they rescue Morning Dew? How could they avenge themselves on Thompson? Both Osceola and John Hawk moved their hands and feet within the confining irons so that the blood could circulate. They did Indian stretching exercises. They spoke of punishing the Emanthlas and the other chiefs who urged the tribes to move west. John Hawk and Osceola would lead the Indians who were willing to fight.

Reason struggled with rage. They sipped stale water and shared the stale bread with the mice. Born to freedom, Osceola felt degraded by being caged. He had been lifted to the most honored, trusted position of the Seminole nation now that Micanopy was an old man and chief in name only.

"We'll survive," Osceola promised.

And what of Morning Dew? What would become of her? Abused, perhaps even murdered by a terrible master. Through the window, John Hawk saw the slender shadows of oleander leaves moving in a soft breeze.

During the second night, a guard's forage cap appeared in the barred window. John Hawk called out, "Guard! Guard!"

The man answered from the safety of the heavy dungeon door. "What?"

"You know this Luis Pacheco, who wants the Indians to accept a third council?"

"Yes, he is slave to Antonio Pacheco."

"Could you get a message to Luis?"

"Sure, he's working here in the fort."

Knowing that Luis was working in the Fort, John Hawk envied him his freedom. Frustrated and full to the throat with fierce hatred for being brought to this condition, John Hawk found his own smell an insult. In a fit of despondency, he wished for death to take him from this stench of urine and decay. Momentarily, his determination to fight sank into a morass of misery.

All night, John's arms and legs tingled with pain, torturing him. He slept fitfully, dreaming frightening dreams. He recalled the terror of racing from Blount's Fort; he heard the cries of the burned and injured and dying.

He dreamed of Osceola dragging canoes of refugees into the jungle and covering them with shrubs and dry leaves. In his nightmares, a tenderness swept John Hawk as he remembered Osceola telling Morning Dew that "Indian girls don't cry."

John awoke with a start. Where was Morning Dew now? His depression was as hard as a rock. Through the bars of the narrow window of the dungeon, he could see a full moon flooding the earth with white light. Never had a moon seemed more beautiful to John Hawk.

Osceola said, "I hope my Morning Dew sees that moon too." Both men watched the shining moon for as long as it remained within the framework of the barred window. Then they began again to flex their arms and legs and arch their backs.

"What a rotten taste in my mouth," Osceola said.

John wondered if he could survive another day. For three days and three nights they had had only a small amount of food and water. Outside the fort, Seminoles milled around threateningly, armed, doing war dances. The sound of war drums could be heard in the dungeon.

At last the door of the dungeon swung open, and John Hawk recognized Luis. "Osceola . . . John . . . are you all right?" He had brought a bottle of water and some oranges.

He knelt and with an iron key released the wrist and ankle chains. "I came as soon as I could." Stiff and aching, hardly able to sit up, John crawled across the slimy floor and grabbed an iron bar to pull himself to his feet. Osceola, moaning, took only a few steps before he had to stop weakly to lean against the door frame.

"More than fifteen hundred Indians have surrounded the Fort," Luis said. "They won't leave until you are released."

Luis got between the two men and helped support them as

he led them by a back path to the wooden steps of the porch where the general's guards took over, ushering them into Thompson's office.

There was nothing but enmity in Thompson's eyes as he studied the two filthy, half-starved men: Osceola had been in chains four days, John more than three. John's odor came to his nostrils as an insult. His arms and legs were covered with dried blood and black and blue bruises. Osceola's wrists were lacerated, his ankles bloody and torn. His early struggles against the irons had left deep cuts.

Thompson rose. "You can go." The men started to leave, but Thompson had more to say, "I ask you again to sign this paper saying the Treaty of Payne's Landing is valid."

"No use," Osceola said.

Thompson, in a quandary, knew if he did not release John Hawk and Osceola, he risked the lives of all who lived in the Fort. The Indians' drums beat out a war dance.

Osceola struggled out to the porch. John followed, flinging himself with pain on Sam. Osceola jumped on a thick mare, and as the American troops watched in sullen silence, an ominous cloud seemed to hang over the Fort. Osceola turned the horse toward the gates of the Fort, crying, "Remember the hour! The sun is high! The agent had his hour! I'll have mine!"

At the edge of the Fort, he turned his mare so suddenly, it veered in the air, lifting its front legs. Osceola let loose a blood-curdling Seminole war cry: "Yo-heeeee-ho!"

No one who heard that cry ever forgot it.

16

During the three days that John Hawk was imprisoned, Sam had not been properly fed, watered, nor rubbed down. John Hawk felt the horse growing weak beneath him.

At a brook in the deep forest, John Hawk and Osceola drew up their mounts. The men jumped down to bathe and drink. Osceola wallowed in the stream and drank in big gulps as if to cleanse himself inside and out. Flinging his wet, dirty clothes form him, he scrubbed his body with clean sand from the bottom of the brook. Revived, and optimistic again, he hung his clothes to dry on a tree limb. "What news of Morning Dew?"

John Hawk was surprised that Osceola had refrained from asking sooner. "Didn't you hear that guard tell you?"

"I was so upset I didn't hear anything."

"He said your wife is safe. Home in the hammock."

Osceola slapped his forehead. "What a fool I am! I knew that guard was trying to tell me something. I wouldn't admit I knew English."

"You were angry," John Hawk said. "Who could blame you?" He splashed in the running brook, reveling in the cold water. "Hadjo caught up with the slave catchers near Fort Brooke. He and Cudjo ransomed your wife."

Naked and wet, John wandered about picking mushrooms and berries. In the hot April sun, the two Indian chiefs lay on the grass in the shade of a mulberry tree, eating and waiting for their ragged clothes to dry.

Then, wearing still-damp trousers, they mounted the horses again. Sam seemed refreshed by the water and the rest in the cool shade. John Hawk headed for Pacheco's plantation, where they might get food and spend a few quiet hours before returning to Cuscowilla.

"Luis is away," Pacheco told John Hawk. John had never before met Luis's master and he liked him immediately—the frank, flashing black eyes and the Spanish olive skin.

Pacheco, a reasonable and religious man, said, "I'm glad to have you and Osceola here for as long as you wish."

"I have to get home to my wife. But we'd appreciate a meal and some food to carry."

After they had eaten, John drew aside two slaves he had known many years. "Why do Luis live in the Fort?" he asked.

"He be guide. He be interpreter for Army."

Luis, doing the white man's business? How could he? John Hawk's gall rose at the idea. The slaves seemed envious. Antonio Pacheco admitted he received twenty-five dollars a month for Luis's services in leading government troops through the Everglades. "And Luis gets paid the same amount," Pacheco said. A princely sum for a slave.

Impatiently, Osceola put a stop to the talk. An old woman wished Luis had not gone to the Fort. "Luis," she explained, "he read papers from up north. We learn what happen. He read papers from Spain. Now no one tell us nothin'. . ."

John Hawk felt like two people in his head were having a fight. After all, Luis had been the one to free Osceola and John. But if Luis had joined the white cause, he was a traitor to his own people. Sick at heart, John Hawk packed for the trip; bread, cabbage, tomatoes, oranges, cheese. He and Osceola loaded up their horses and set out for Cuscowilla. One thought was on his mind: vengeance. In the course of the years, John Hawk had never forgotten the massacre of Blount's Fort. The long walk back from the West had left him bitter and disillusioned after seeing the terrible land that was to become Indian Territory. Time after time, the white man had betrayed the Indians. But John Hawk believed that if there was a war, it would not be an Indian war but a runaways war, and the plantation owners would feel the effects of it on their slave populations.

After a week of rest at home with Morning Dew, Osceola called his friends to his chickee for a powwow. He talked about the Emanthlas. No Indian would join Osceola in an act of revenge against other Indians. John Hawk and Negro Abraham, assuming the roles of runaways protecting the interest of other runaways, agreed to go with Osceola to Emanthlas' village.

Charlie Emanthla knew why Osceola had come with two famous friends and warriors. Osceola had plainly announced that the first chief who accepted emigration must die. Charlie Emanthla ran to his father's chickee shouting, "Hurry, hurry, hide in the forest! Hide!"

The old man moved slowly, gathering a blanket about him, pushing his feet into moccasins and walking feebly toward the woods, his head shaking, his limbs trembling.

Then Charlie came toward the three approaching Seminoles on horseback. Osceola was recognizable from the distance for his straight stance and egret feathers in his turban, and the other two men, inches taller, Negro Abraham and John Hawk. Charlie and John Hawk had often smoked a peace pipe or shared a rabbit over an open fire.

As their horses stirred up the dust with their fast trot, John Hawk played the role of peacemaker. "Osceola, do not do this. It is a mistake. Don't kill Charlie."

Osceola did not greet Charlie by gesture or words. His face seemed carved of stone. The younger Emanthla carried a peace pipe.

Charlie Emanthla spoke first. "Osceola, we are not enemies. The settlers are our enemies."

"You have lost faith with your black brothers," Osceola replied.

"My black brothers live among us as friends and family. They must migrate with us to the new lands."

"But you would go where there are slave catchers," Osceola said angrily, his arms folded across his chest.

"Slave catchers everywhere," Charlie replied. "I heard about what happened to Morning Dew. I offer my regret."

"Eat your regret," Osceola responded.

Charlie gestured for them to sit down around the flaming campfire. The women had corn, husk and all, roasting in the hot coals, the sweet fragrance filling the air. John refused to eat. He could not accept hospitality from a man he might have to kill. Abraham and Charlie snatched ears of corn from the fire and smeared the kernels with bear grease.

Charlie held an ear of corn. He argued, "We have no hope for a good life here. At least in the West we can hunt and fish."

Osceola replied, "We won't leave. They will drive us west and then drive us from the lands there again. Somewhere we have to make a stand."

"Not here," Charlie said, wiping his mouth with the back of his hand and throwing what was left of his corn back into the fire. "We will all be killed."

The word "killed" hung in the air like a stink. The talk continued, hard and earnest. Charlie would not budge. He did not want his women and children murdered by the whites. The war was stupid. If the Indians resisted, they would all die or become slaves. If he had to give his own life to save theirs, so be it.

"Will you agree to resist the white man here in your own village? Will you just agree to remain here?" Osceola pressed him.

"No. We will all die," Charlie said strongly. John Hawk's heart was heavy as Osceola raised his rifle.

Abraham, with a quick motion, shoved the rifle upward so it aimed at the sky. "You do not kill a brother."

Time was running out. Osceola had many promises to keep. Abraham said, "Kill one of your own and you wound yourself."

Osceola replied, "We cannot stand divided. The Seminoles

will disappear as a nation if we do not resist this migration. The first to surrender breaks the back of the nation."

Charlie Emanthla drew his blanket closer around him and rose, calm as the rising of the moon. He recognized his fate and was ready to meet it. Osceola fired. The shot echoed and reechoed, to be heard to the very edge of all the land of the Seminoles. Emanthla dropped his blanket and stood, blood running down his chest and legs. Wearing only a loin cloth, his body unpainted, a man who would not yield from his convictions, he held up both hands. "I live," he said in quiet agony, "I still live." Then he fell backward.

Osceola fired again. Emanthla lay still as a statue.

Attached to a beaded belt that supported Charlie's loincloth were bags of gold and silver coins he had received for the sale of his cattle, in preparation for moving west. Osceola opened the bags. He took a handful of gold and glanced at the silent judging faces of Emanthla's people who had come in response to the shooting. Before the frightened eyes of the children, he felt a moment of guilt.

Oh, Great Spirit, what have I done? Osceola had killed a brother in cold blood. Was it right? Could it ever be right?

Osceola threw the coins in all directions. "No one is to touch this dirty gold. This is the price Charlie took for his brothers' blood."

Osceola scattered the coins contemptuously. The children stared at the bright gold and silver glittering in the sun, but none reached to pick one up.

John Hawk, Osceola, and Abraham sat down near the fire, their arms crossed on their chests. No one moved to bury Emanthla. When darkness fell, Holata Emanthla led his tribe from the camp. Women carried household packs on their backs. The few horses that had not been sold were loaded with blankets and baskets. Little children held what their arms could support. The tribe departed by the flickering firelight, single file into the deep, dark woods. John heard the sibilant sounds of

whispered commands and the weeping of women, the long silences, broken only by the movement of horses and Indians.

Many months later, John Hawk was in the forest nearby and suddenly came upon the abandoned chickees of the Emanthla tribe. There lay the slain Charlie Emanthla, his bones bleaching in the sun. Nearby the gold coins still glittered. No one had touched them.

17

The grey dawn crept into the chickee. John Hawk stirred. Chumpee put a reassuring hand on his back.

"Sleep a little longer," she urged quietly.

"I'm not sleeping," John Hawk growled. "I'm fretting."

"Well, fret a little longer," she chuckled.

"I did not like the killing of Emanthla," John reflected soberly. "Now Osceola talks of nothing but revenge on Thompson."

"Morning Dew should stop that talk."

"No one can change Osceola's mind."

"Are you going away today?"

"Osceola wants me to take work at the Fort so I can watch Thompson. The Fort is hiring."

Chumpee rose to build a fire. She brewed sassafras tea. Morning Dew came and knelt by the glowing coals and drank some tea.

During the morning, Chumpee and Morning Dew collected palm leaves for a new roof for Osceola's chickee. When they returned in the evening with baskets of leaves, Osceola chided them. "You gone long enough!"

Chumpee saw that he and Morning Dew had quarreled. Morning Dew muttered something under her breath. Osceola replied, "A squaw does not interfere in the business of her brave."

Morning Dew, her black eyes flashing, replied, "This is my business too."

Chumpee was pleased to see Morning Dew's spirit. "I do not want to be a widow," Morning Dew insisted.

Osceola replied, "It is better to die with courage than live as a coward."

"Wrong," Morning Dew replied. "Life offers many chances for courage. Death only one."

John Hawk came to Osceola's chickee and began to cover the old roof with the fresh palm leaves. Osceola, helping him, asked, "Did you get to the Fort to see if they have a job for you?"

John Hawk hated the idea of spying, but he remembered favors Osceola had done him. "The Fort is hiring runaways to do jobs that the lowest private won't do."

"Take the job," Osceola insisted. John Hawk knew that his friend's soul was preoccupied with vengeance; Osceola nursed his wounds with a passion. "I dreamed last night," Osceola said, "that I had fired the gun that killed Thompson."

John Hawk went cold at the idea of another murder.

The next morning, John Hawk lined up for work in the Fort. Not one full-blood Indian waited in line. Many applicants were coffee-colored like himself, some were mixed black and Indian, some very black. The hiring agent called out, "Anyone who reads and writes?"

"I can!" John Hawk responded, the single voice raised.

"Step forward!" The rest of the men were sent away.

John reported to a room full of opened boxes of books. He had been hired to help set up a library. Stanley Smith, an officer from New Jersey was a small man with smooth hands and clean fingernails. As he and John unpacked the books, Smith said, "I'm impressed by your efficiency."

John gave him a toothy fake smile. To a white man, a black who could read and write was a phenomenon. But one who could also work efficiently was a marvel.

John found himself suddenly happy. Sunlight poured in at

the open windows as he sorted books and filed magazines that had been shipped from Washington. Every time a magazine fell open, John became absorbed in reading. When Lt. Smith spoke to him, John, guiltily, would put the magazine on its proper shelf, trying to remember where he had put it so he could get back to finish the article.

John Hawk observed, not without bitterness, "How do you expect my people to be literate if you don't allow us to learn? And how do you expect us to be efficient if you treat us like animals?"

Abashed, the lieutenant said, "I want you to know I am opposed to slavery." He flushed crimson. "Here, let me help you with that set of encyclopedias."

Together they unpacked the heavy volumes and lined them up on the shelf, A – Z.

"Attention!" A corporal at the door saluted. Two men entered, General Thompson and a gray-haired civilian. John Hawk went stiff as a ramrod, his spine turning to ice. The reaction was not to seeing Thompson and knowing he was spying on him, but at the recognition of the elderly man in the frock coat. His father! His own father and master! He had not seen his father in twenty years. He had been thirteen years old when he ran away from the plantation. Yet John recognized his father at once. Would the father know the son?

The elderly man took a step toward John Hawk, a puzzled frown and surprised expression behind the proffered handshake. The old man could not be sure that John Hawk was not black. A Southern gentleman never shook hands with a black man.

"You look so familiar!" the old man exclaimed, part statement, part question.

"All darkies look alike," John Hawk immediately regretted his sarcasm. It was dangerous to be flippant in front of Thompson. John could find himself back in the dungeon, or worse.

Thompson asked the librarian if the assistant was working out. Smith replied, "John Hawk's a good worker."

Thompson said, "John Hawk, you could earn your salary if you found an explanation for the disappearing ammunition from the post."

The lieutenant said, "Please don't ask him to spy."

Thompson went rigid with rage. "Everyone on the Fort must be alert to ammunition being stolen."

The old man said, "My name is John White, and I'm searching for my only son who has the same name. Have you ever heard of him?"

Twenty years had passed. Had his father spent two decades searching for a runaway son? If so, why? To return him to slavery? To leave him an inheritance? To repay injustices? To salve his own conscience?

John turned to hide his tears. He was deeply moved, and frightened. He could hardly stand erect. His legs trembled.

His father had never mistreated him. His father had taught him to read the Bible and to write letters. John Hawk recalled times as a little boy when his father had taken him on his knees and read him stories. This time of year, near Christmas, the stories about Old Saint Nicholas, Santa Claus, Baby Jesus, Daniel in the Lion's Den, and Joseph and his brothers all came back to John Hawk. Like himself, his father had been a victim of the mores and morals of the times. A black woman might be truly loved, but a white man could not marry her nor legitimize her children.

"My wife and daughter died in an epidemic two years ago," John White said, "and I came to St. Augustine to see if I might find my son and make him my heir. Strange," mused the old man with the watery blue eyes, "I feel as if we've met before. Were you ever in Georgia, John Hawk?" He said the name as if exploring his memory.

John Hawk longed to see his mother again. "Would your son have to live in Georgia to claim an inheritance?" John Hawk asked, his voice shaking.

Thompson, suddenly watching John Hawk keenly, asked severely, "Do you know this John White? If you do, stop beating around the bush and tell us where he can be found."

"I know of no man who calls himself by that name," John Hawk replied. He did not want to inherit property that had become rich and fertile through the sweat and blood of his black brothers. Now he belonged to the Indians and was a Seminole chief. He reminded himself of his mission here: to spy on General Thompson.

18

In the fort library, John Hawk helped a soldier decorate a small pine tree with strings of popcorn.

"Major Dade and his troops will leave Fort Brooke on the twenty-fifth," the soldier said.

John Hawk kept his face as expressionless as an Indian's. These soldiers know nothing of military security, he thought. Lieutenant Smith exclaimed, "Christmas Day! Peace on earth! Go out to kill Indians!"

Smith brought a load of books for John to catalog. The officer was so short he had to cut inches off his regulation trousers. "You could be a librarian. God knows you're smart enough."

For a wild moment, John almost confessed to this friendly man that in his presence, in this very room, he had denied his own father.

John Hawk's soul had been in torment since he had seen his father. Old memories, not all of them sad, haunted him. He recalled how slaves had been given special food and a day of music and merrymaking on Christmas. He had loved the small tree decorated with eggshells saved by the cooks. John had had his first taste of an orange one Christmas morning. His mother had been allowed to come from her master's plantation and had brought him a blanket and an orange, gifts to her from her master. But all those happy memories had to be suppressed. Something more important was happening now.

At midnight on December 23, John met Osceola at their appointed place outside the wall of the dungeon. John had given Osceola a box of stolen ammunition. John sensed that the kidnapping of Osceola's wife had been as great a shock as his imprisonment, and he tried to get Osceola to talk about it. Osceola confessed to feeling miserable, and said he was suffering from having murdered Emanthla. "Troubled conscience" were words John's father had used, but Indians usually did not speak of such ideas.

Lieutenant Smith lit a few candles on the small tree. "Looks festive," he said. John agreed.

"How about breakfast?" Smith indicated a chair at a table in front of the blazing fireplace. John hesitated.

"Come on," urged Smith, pouring coffee into two mugs. The silver of the coffee pot reflected the red flames in the firelight. This was the nicest time of year at the fort, the weather neither too hot nor too humid.

John could not resist the fragrance of the coffee. He liked the smell of it better than the taste. Sitting down opposite Smith, he said, "Well, Merry Christmas."

The lieutenant scooped some scrambled eggs and pieces of bacon on a plate and offered John hot biscuits. "Same to you," Smith said. "I wish I could figure out what our government is thinking about. Hundreds of forts built in Florida, thousands of miles cleared, thousands of soldiers here against a handful of Seminoles."

John's eyes widened at Smith's frankness. He had never expected to hear a white man express that viewpoint. He felt a kinship with the officer. White man, black man, Indian chief, what's the difference? We all have a common humanity, we all hope for peace.

He finished the breakfast with pleasure. A thin nervous man wearing thick glasses came into the room. Lieutenant Smith introduced John Hawk to Ransome Clark, whose uniform hung on him, looking as if he were wearing someone else's castoffs. Ransome Clark joined them in front of the fire. An old soldier came to the door. "Ain't you got nothing to do, nigger? Go chop wood."

John Hawk rose and went out to his cot, where he had his father's ax hidden in his duffle bag. As he chopped wood, Ransome Clark came along, like a friendly puppy looking for a boy to adopt. John had hardly struck the first log when the head of the ax flew off its handle. Ransome laughed. "Here, he took the split handle from John. "I'll fix that for you." He picked up the ax head. "No harm done. Come to the tool shed and I'll make you a new handle."

Sure enough, Ransome Clark found a new hickory handle, a piece of wood with a beautiful grain. Though the ax head did not fit exactly, Clark had a lathe and a turning wood machine and he made the top of the handle more narrow. Why wasn't Clark preparing to leave Fort King? The horses and wagons waited to take him and his tools. Mesmerized by his friendliness, John thought Clark treated him as an equal. John watched the small, skillful hands turn the top of the wood handle until it fit the ax precisely. With a heavy mallet, Clark whacked the ax head into place. Good as new!

John Hawk, eager to get out of the Fort, needed to count the soldiers Dade led into the forest. Osceola had to know the size of the regiment. John Hawk learned that the Seminoles had attacked three boatloads of corn coming down the St. Johns River from Georgia. Seventeen soldiers had been wounded, two killed. The Seminoles now had taken not only much corn but many wagons laden with supplies. The Indians and blacks who hid in the swamps and forests struck with lightning speed. Smith told John Hawk, "These war tactics were never taught at West Point."

Taking his ax, John picked up a bag of coffee sitting on a wagon that had been packed for maneuvers. He headed for the yard just as a drummer beat a long roll warning the last laggards to fall in.

Three officers turned out of the ranks and trotted smartly on handsome horses around the clearing. A woman cried, "Kill some savages for me!"

Civilians broke into a round of applause, as cheerful as the sunny morning. Major Dade had a perfect day to set out on his mission. The sun was warm. Dade, like an actor in a play, wore glamorous silver epaulets on broad shoulders, his black boots highly polished resting in silver stirrups. His uniform was new. From the rifle boot slung on his saddle, his doublebarreled shotgun projected. His great curled cavalry saber hung below his left hip, the gleaming silver grip matching the embroidered silver horn on his coat.

"*Forward, Ho!*" Major Dade sang the command. Women and children ran forward for a last hug from their soldiers. Here and there, a uniformed man lifted a child to urge him to be brave. A little blond boy smothered sobs as he rubbed tearful eyes.

"Bye, Papa!" His mother stepped forward to rescue him from the horses' nervous hooves. John Hawk stayed back, his eyes searching for Luis. The soldiers marched from the Fort with cries of "Merry Christmas!" Two uneven columns of soldiers with black forage caps lifting and falling soon disappeared into the rich green foliage which rustled as the men passed, their boots crushing the rain frost beneath their feet.

High in the pines, cardinals and bluebirds scolded and fluttered. The fragrance of crushed pine needles filled the air. An ox-team moved slowly out of the gate, the driver upon the wagon coaxing, goading. The wagon was full of food, blankets, ammunition, medicine, and barrels of water. At the very rear, Ransome Clark on his horse-driven wagon of tools urged the animal forward. Sitting with his legs dangling from the side of the wagon was Luis, the sole black man with the troops.

John made the Seminole sign of "Good luck!" Luis lifted an eyebrow almost imperceptibly in response.

John took off through the deep forest to the hammock

where Osceola had led the Seminoles. Chumpee, overjoyed to see John Hawk, warned, "Watch for the bear trap! Come," she said, taking his hand.

Morning Dew had a rabbit on a spit. Osceola, Wild Cat, and John Hawk ate and did war talk. First, Osceola insisted, there had to be revenge on Thompson. He could no longer wait. Then the Seminoles would follow the troops to the ten willows near Great Wahoo to ambush the troops.

John spoke against killing Thompson. He was carrying the very rifle Thompson had given him, and he was afraid that the death of Thompson would bring down the wrath of the whole government on the Seminoles.

"What else have we known but wrath?" Osceola cried, pointing to the scars on his ankles. "To chain an Indian is to degrade him."

"Forgive Thompson," John Hawk insisted.

"That's white man's talk," Osceola declared. "The red man seeks vengeance. The spirits of the dead do not rest until they are avenged."

Wild Cat sat behind Chumpee and braided silver ornaments into his twin sister's hair. As a child, Chumpee had often worn white doeskin. But now white was too impractical Like the other Seminole women, Chumpee wore skirts made of strips of rags sewn into patchwork.

She liked Wild Cat to braid her hair. Every once in a while, she stole a glance at John Hawk to show her joy that he was near.

"O-ko-to?" Chumpee offered her husband a bowl of wild radishes. He ate with pleasure, his teeth crunching on the white and red tartness.

"We know Thompson walks every day now from the fort to the sutler's," Osceola said. Harry Roberts, the sutler, ran a small store selling liquor, candy, tobacco, and playing cards to soldiers.

After they ate, John Hawk, Osceola, and Wild Cat moved through the forest, disappearing against thick trunks of trees, hardly rustling the leaves of a shrub, making no sounds as they stepped on the underbrush. With loaded rifles, they found an area of wild bushes from which they could see the path leading from the Fort to the house which was both home and store for Roberts. John and Osceola lay prone in the deep concealing grass, while Wild Cat climbed a tree, his rifle aimed.

The first clue they had of Thompson's approach was the smell of his cigar smoke. Then they heard footsteps and conversation.

John, lifting his head, saw Thompson walking with old John White. John's heart constricted and he muttered, "Don't shoot!" At this moment, both Wild Cat and Osceola aimed their rifles. John heard his father say that Dade and his men should be near the swamp. Both Indians fired at once, so that first shot sounded as one, and then a rain of bullets followed. Thompson fell forward, blood streaming out of him in half a dozen places. John White, riddled too, died immediately. The shrill war whoop following the crack of rifles could be heard for miles around: *Yo-ho-heee-ho!*

John Hawk had no heart for violence. He had a harsh, horrible vision of shooting himself and being found in the deep woods near his father's body. John lay in the tall weeds, his head pounding. He would not move until the bodies were taken back to the fort for a decent burial. The smell of the weeds scratched his sinuses. Mosquitoes swarmed around, biting him. Have a picnic, he told them.

When darkness fell, he wondered if he could carry both bodies back to the fort himself. Would the soldiers shoot him on sight? John Hawk knew Osceola was impatient to start out toward Great Wahoo Swamp, where they were to join up with other Indian marauders.

John Hawk hardly realized how much seeing his father again had meant to him. He wished now he had acknowledged him. How happy an hour they might have had together.

Seminoles, with war whoops and high yelps, set the sutler's shop on fire. Two black men he did not recognize ran down the road, their arms full of tobacco and bottles of wine.

At last John Hawk did not dare delay any longer. Rising, he struggled up, his arms and legs stiff and aching. A small group of daring soldiers ran down the road toward the burning shop. John Hawk shouted to them to come carry Thompson's body. John himself went forward to lift the stiff cold form of his father in his arms. With his father's ax still attached to his belt, John Hawk walked the long mile toward the Fort. The gate opened. The guards, recognizing John Hawk as a worker at the fort, did not suspect his role in the recent violence. Smith rushed to help John, thanking him for bringing back the body to the fort. In the woodshed, a pine box was readied. A soldier arranged the body, almost reverently, and the cover was placed on the coffin. With the blunt side of his ax head, John Hawk beat the nails of the cover into place. He hammered twelve long nails into the coffin.

"Honor thy father and thy mother." He remembered his father's lessons on the Ten Commandments. But John thought that love and respect must be earned. His father had sold John's mother to a neighbor. Was such a father to be loved and honored?

John ran through the gate of the Fort and out into the still, starless night.

19

A sense of danger, of impending tragedy more terrible than any he had ever known, had hold of John Hawk. Wild Cat appeared at his chickee. "Ready?" he asked.

Osceola, now known as *tustenuggee thlacko* (commanding officer) had gone on alone. John Hawk and Wild Cat set out through the thick forest in the brutal cold. John's heavy heart seemed a physical burden. He even walked heavily, trodding on thick underbrush and sinking now and then ankle-deep in mud. Ordinarily, he had a light tread, and like an Indian, could go through the forest so softly that even animals were taken by surprise.

John could not get his father out of his mind. Wild Cat rubbed salt into the wound by talking about his own father.

"In a way, King Philip is like Osceola. Not so smart, maybe. He has the same influence in bringing the Seminoles together. Philip will not move west. He says this good land has been ours since the sun first shone here."

King Philip had over 200 former slaves living with him and the St. Johns River Indians. "Philip says the Great Spirit may exterminate us, but the palefaces will not."

The rising sun lit the tops of the trees with a soft golden glow. They came to an Indian hammock where the women were building up campfires to cook the first meal of the day. From the burning embers came the sweet, acrid smell of smoke and roasting ears of corn. Wild Cat and John Hawk stopped for hot sassafras tea and they ate many ears of corn smeared with bear grease. Then an Indian woman offered to take them across the small lake in her canoe.

Getting out of the boat, Wild Cat ran like a deer across the clearing to the forest. John took the time to thank the Indian woman and raced after Wild Cat, who was marvelously agile and swift. Breathless, they walked together through the dark forest, Wild Cat wearing a ferocious expression. His honey-colored skin was like that of his twin, Chumpee.

John thought of Chumpee's face. It was not the face of a sorceress like Hummingbird's, nor of an African princess like Morning Dew's. Chumpee's face, with the high cheekbones and the nose of an Indian, had a smooth brow and wonderful reassuring black eyes. She never laughed loudly, but often giggled with pleasure, and her smile revealed lovely even teeth.

Thinking of her made the morning seem brighter. John Hawk was glad he had the deerskin jacket she had made. He and Wild Cat waded across a stream where water snakes slithered and an alligator flopped its tail warningly. The water was paralyzingly cold.

Hours later they came upon stove-in barrels and broken bottles, evidence that the Seminoles had camped here. They found the remains of a butchered deer, still edible because of the cold. John cut chunks of the half-frozen meat. Wild Cat built a fire, and they put the meat on a spit. Warming themselves close to the flames, they took off their wet moccasins. Wild Cat said there should be a bridge not far away that he remembered the white men building about ten or twelve years earlier. But when they got started again, they found that nothing was as they had expected.

In the lackluster sun, where the bridge had been, only charred embers remained. Smoke rose in the distance. Within a few miles they came over a bluff to the ruined, burned skeleton of a trading post.

At twilight, they were met by Micanopy near the edge of the swamp and guided to the armed and waiting Seminoles. After dark, John climbed a tree and surveyed the temporary barricades erected by the soldiers. He counted over a hundred men within the log breastworks, only a few awake on guard. He felt pity and distress for them. Major Dade slept in a sitting position against a cannon.

Beneath John Hawk, Micanopy moved from tree to tree, his rifle ready. John's imagination turned every tree and shadow into a uniformed sentinel. Once he could have sworn a soldier with a glittering silver buckle stood beneath him, but it was only the moon shining on a piece of glass. John Hawk heard the soldiers coughing or crying out in their sleep, and the whispering of Luis with the sentinels on duty. He could make out Luis's features. Good old Luis. He could always be relied on!

Now, despite his age and heaviness, Micanopy mounted the barricade and dropped inside, going straight for the sleeping Major Dade with a raised knife. Micanopy plunged his knife into the man's heart. The officer never awoke. The fight was on!

From every side, the Indians fired, some from prone positions and some from the trees. Whatever bullets the soldiers shot went over the heads of the Indians or into the brush. John Hawk held his fire. No need to waste ammunition. A rain of bullets poured into Major Dade, already dead.

As stealthily as a snake slithers along the ground, Wild Cat pulled himself up the tree beside John. Taking careful aim, he fired. Within the breastwork, many soldiers were dead before they could reach their guns, and many more were wounded. The dazed soldiers, crazed with fear, struggled to get out of the barricades. Some lay dead, half in and half out of the useless breastworks.

His heart pounding, sickened by the violence, John Hawk reminded himself that he was an Indian chief. His sympathies in war with the Indians could not wipe out his sense of outrage at the pain and plight of the poor soldiers. Groans of agony came from within the breastworks. How pitiable and trapped the soldiers were! John Hawk suffered a sense of being too powerful.

When John saw the familiar wiry black head of Luis beneath him, he dropped to embrace his friend. Within the barricades, among the few soldiers remaining alive, Ransome Clark helped a doctor stretch a blanket across pine saplings to cradle a bleeding man. John Hawk hoped the thin, bespectacled toolmaker would be spared. A bullet killed the man on the stretcher.

John Hawk had no idea how long the Indians had been firing into the barricades. High-pitched yelps and war whoops filled the air with fear.

"Yo-ho-heeeeeee!!" screamed Alligator, firing into the barricades. Osceola echoed the frightening scream and, at last, gave the signal for the Indians to withdraw. With fiendish yells, the braves mounted the soldiers' horses, leading away those few they had brought of their own, and they rode off.

John delayed departure, intending to rescue Ransome Clark. Within the hastily constructed barricades, few signs of life remained. A few runaways were drinking the soldiers' liquor rations.

John Hawk recognized a dead soldier whom he had known at Fort King, a German who had told John that in the German army he had been given 300 lashes for trying to desert. Why had he, escaping to the New World, joined an army again? The German had longed to be a shoemaker, and had promised himself he would never again join an army.

That poor soldier was one of many who had seen service in the Irish, British, Scotch, or Polish armies, and the German claimed they were all good military men. But as humans, they were brutalized. No wife, no family, no home, no roots. Fighting Indians in Florida had dehumanized them even more.

Summers they were bitten raw by insects, crawled over in their sleep by roaches, attacked by snakes; winters they were dizzy with dysentery, shivering in makeshift camps. John Hawk had seen them at Fort King, almost dead with fatigue.

When John Hawk found Ransome Clark, lying on his back, glasses askew, face bloody, he knelt beside him and asked, "Can you hear me?" He touched the soldier's skin; it was warm. Ransome lifted a weak hand. John offered a drink from a canteen to the thin man. Gratefully, Clark drank.

A number of blacks still wandered around within the barricades, knifing half-dead men. John Hawk rose and, holding up his hands, cried, "Do not pillage! Leave this place at once. Don't let the world think Seminoles fight for plunder! Leave the money and watches here." With this, the blacks departed with the remaining arms.

"Can you stand up?" John asked.

"Hit in the legs," Ransome said.

John lifted Clark and carried him to the barricades, where he laid him down. He pulled himself over the barricade, then lifted Clark into his arms and set out across the clumps of frozen palmettos and tall wiregrass.

Near a frozen stream, John Hawk helped Clark lie down. John built a fire so they could get warm. Then he lay on his stomach with his loaded rifle, watching for wolves, partridge, or small game. Aiming at a rabbit whose pink eyes seemed to gaze straight at him as if to make friends, he shot it between its big ears. He skinned the rabbit and rolled up the fur to take to Chumpee. Then roasted the rabbit over the fire and shared the meat with Ransome Clark.

"How can I thank you?" Clark asked.

"Forget it," John Hawk said.

Just then a riderless horse appeared. John jumped up and gave the horse a wild chase. The horse almost escaped, but John managed to catch it by its halter and jump on its back. He rode it back to where Clark lay exhausted.

"Can you ride it back to Fort King?"

"If I don't get lost."

"Good luck."

John Hawk helped Clark up to the back of the horse and gave the rump a smart slap. Off galloped the horse, with the wounded Clark bouncing on top. Poor fellow was in for a jostling ride. But he would survive.

Picking up his ax and rifle, John Hawk set out for King Philip's village. Before long, he spotted a figure on a horse silhouetted against the sky, now dappled with seaborne clouds. John Hawk fell into the bushes, hiding from the approaching rider. The figure became recognizable: Osceola!

John rose and raised an arm. Osceola, sighting him, made an answering gesture. John's heart lifted. Osceola spurred his horse to a trot and was soon within hailing distance. "John Hawk!" he cried, his voice uncharacteristic of an Indian — excited.

He gestured to John Hawk to mount the horse behind him. With a running leap, John was up behind Osceola. They rode back to their wives in silence, each pursuing private thoughts.

20

In the American press, the defeat at Great Wahoo Swamp was called a massacre. To the Seminoles, the attack was a great victory. In Florida, armed and ready for war, the Seminoles recalled Blount's Fort, and at last felt avenged for their martyred dead.

John Hawk, back at Fort King, carrying a spade as if he were on a job, walked into the infirmary the day he learned Ransome Clark was to have surgery. John had checked on Clark several times and had worried about his gunshot wound. The surgeon, preparing to remove bullets from Clark's foot, said he would have to remove a couple of small bones.

Clark made eye contact with John Hawk and quipped, "You think they'd make good soup?"

John breathed a sigh of relief. If Clark could joke that way, he was going to be all right, crusty fellow.

Clark and Luis were the only survivors of those who had been within the barracks. Luis continued to present a friendly face to the whites. He and Negro Abraham were known as "friendlies." But Luis visited regularly at the Seminole chickees hidden deep in the forests. He brought food from Pacheco's plantation, and bananas, plantains, yams, and tobacco from the Cubans, with whom he was now trading. "I'm a free man," Luis told John Hawk.

Osceola's son had been born in December, and Luis brought

milk to the child. The Seminoles suffered terribly in the bitter cold winter. They had lost their homes and crops. The squaws walked miles to pick corn, kernel by kernel, that had been dropped by horses. Indian cattle had been destroyed by the white settlers. Indian women washed old corn or flour sacks to make clothing for themselves and the children. Every scrap of material discarded by the whites was sewn and resewn into patchwork skirts, shirts, or pants.

Things were not much better for the army. Civilians and military were running short of provisions. Unlike the Indians who could survive on palmetto cabbage, coontie and small game, the soldiers needed supplies from the north.

After Dade's defeat, sentinels, placed thickly around army forts, wore forage clothing, discarding the old shining silver belt buckles and buttons that had made them a target. Even officers dressed like privates. A small lace shoulder strap worn by General Clinch was his only distinction in dress.

Luis reported that soldiers were too nervous to stand watch for the regulation four hours. A soldier who wanted to desert the army asked John Hawk if he would guide him out of Florida, and John Hawk provided the man with a rough map. The next day he was gone.

At night, howling hungry wolves and croaking bullfrogs sent the soldiers at Fort King into panic. Thompson's replacement, little one-armed Colonel Fanning, had expected that all the Seminoles would have gone to the West Country by now. When his enlisted men's terms ran out, few reenlisted.

Chumpee baked corn cakes and roasted rabbits. John Hawk no longer trusted Negro Abraham, who sat cross-legged in the chickee and had very little to say.

King Philip insisted that Indians would have to set up a stronghold even deeper in the swamps. He suggested a possible site some miles from the Kissimmee River.

"It is time for Wild Cat to be chief," Philip said. "Wild Cat's mother is a sister of Micanopy. That unites my tribe to his."

John Hawk considered Wild Cat one of the most able and brave of the Seminoles, next only to Osceola. He agreed that Wild Cat should be a chief, as he glanced from Wild Cat to his twin, the two so alike even their voices had the same inflections.

John watched Chumpee setting food before Osceola and Negro Abraham, her movements graceful, her patchwork skirt fitting her hips smoothly, a white egret feather in her shining black hair. The firelight glowed on her honey-colored skin, and her almond-shaped eyes met and held his. To him, she seemed like a flower in bloom.

Luis read aloud the editorial in the paper about President Andrew Jackson. Jackson could not understand the Seminoles. Ordered to go west, the Indians ignored the order. And the blacks, ordered to return to their masters, had just disobeyed. Now the Creeks were good Indians, according to President Jackson. He told Creeks to go west, and westward they obediently went.

Gen. Thomas Jesup was the third general to take command in Florida. He was another of Jackson's favorites.

"Jesup's a Virginian, cool, steady," Luis said. "He pushed the Creeks into Indian Territory out west. Now he's in Florida. He may send troops into the swamps, and he'll recruit Creeks to help him. He promised the right to sell blacks to every Creek who helped him."

John Hawk's heart sank. He saw Abraham's downcast eyes. Where could the old black man's loyalties lie? A man has to have self-interest and not be put in danger of being sold into slavery.

John Hawk ordered a war dance to celebrate the victory at Wahoo Swamp, and Osceola had the medicine chief arrange a scalp dance. Ordinarily, John Hawk was not a drinking man, but tonight he passed around a bottle of whiskey and, imitating the voice and manners of Wiley Thompson, said, "The Indians who do not go peaceably, the Great White Father will remove by force!"

The men laughed—Negro Abraham, Osceola, Wild Cat, and King Philip. But John Hawk found that laughter did not come easily, because he had hated the murder of the soldiers at Wahoo Swamp. And he had seen his own father murdered. How long could the killing go on? He hoped to see peace in his lifetime.

The hammock where John Hawk now made his home was halfway between Fort Brooke and Fort King. From this community, John Hawk kept track of the movements of the American troops. Blacks kept guard on roads and reported to John Hawk.

General Jesup had suggested the use of bloodhounds. He was eager to do anything to bring the war to an end. At the Fort, John Hawk learned that Jesup had suggested that the Indians be allowed to settle in an area and plant a crop in apparent security. When they were off-guard, Jesup would attack swiftly and either wipe out the Indians or force them to migrate as prisoners.

Now the Seminoles moved again, this time to a chain of islets running from swamp to swamp, near Kissimmee River. The aquatic jungle was well-hidden from the world by fallen trees, heavy brush, and old melon vines. The cypress swamp had clean water, fish, and wild onions. In the dense shadows of tall cypress and pines, the water, infested with alligators and snakes, terrorized the soldiers but yielded sustenance to the Indians.

In the cold winter, the Seminoles felt safe, wrapped in rabbit fur, hunting and foraging for food beneath the thick underbrush. We will survive, John Hawk promised his wife. We will endure.

21

At midnight in his chickee, John Hawk, awakened by approaching footsteps, sat up, alert and listening.

"Who's there?"

"Black Dirt."

John Hawk put a reassuring hand on his wife and whispered, "Honey-girl, I'll be back in a minute." He rolled out of his blanket and pulled on his rabbit jacket and fur pants against the January cold.

"Where are you going?" Chumpee stirred.

"Don't worry." She clung momentarily to his hand, and he spoke reassuringly. Down the road in the dark shadows, Black Dirt whispered alarmingly, "Troops and Creeks are attacking our village on Lake Ahpopka."

Black Dirt, nephew of Chief Osuchee, had been reared at Ahpopka. Osuchee had been one of the leaders at the Battle of Wahoo Swamp. At the edge of the river, four men mounted on horses waited, and John Hawk climbed on Sam while Black Dirt mounted behind him. The horses carefully picked their way over the thick underbrush.

Black Dirt said, "Jesup is going after Osceola."

"How old is Jesup?" John Hawk grunted.

"Fifty," Black Dirt replied.

"That's old enough."

"I'm fifty," Black Dirt said.

John Hawk wondered if he would ever live to see fifty. He thought of the things that he loved, his wife, Sam, Osceola and his family, the summer sun, swimming, the full moon, stars in the sky, the smell of pines, roast corn, wild strawberries.

As the four riders approached Lake Ahpopka through the cypress swamp, dawn turned the surface of the water to a golden, glistening mirror. Beyond the lake, among the last of the unhidden hammocks, the village looked peaceful and pretty, Indian platforms with thatched roofs and wells carefully roofed. The horses trotted between gardens of winter squash and yams. Chickens, pigs, and dogs ran between the horses' legs. Winter corn waved in the thin cold wind. How could you look on this tranquil sleeping village as a battlefield?

The Seminoles had protected their tomatoes by building wind shelters around the vines. Now the red fruit hung like ornaments, and a small lemon tree was heavy with yellow fruit. Squaws came to greet the six men, and soon the children with corncob dolls came shyly to John Hawk.

John climbed to the highest point in the village on top of Osuchee's roof. In the distance he could see the trees moving and now and then a forage cap, and soon an enormous crowd of Creeks and soldiers came into view. Their numbers were far greater than those of the Seminoles in the village. The Seminoles were armed and ready. John Hawk quickly led the rounded-up black families out of the village to a storehouse on a sedgy lagoon at some distance.

With his rifle, he rushed back to the village alone to see Black Dirt and his uncle, Osuchee, carrying white flags, walking toward the oncoming troops to surrender the doomed village. Behind them, the Seminoles watched anxiously. Osuchee was the same height and walked with the same stride as his nephew, Black Dirt. There was a strong family resemblance.

Suddenly, two shots rang out. Both men fell forward, blood spurting out of them. At that, gunfire came from the woods, chickees, and storage buildings. The approaching uniformed battalions scattered into the shadows and behind trees. For hours, the shooting continued and the fighting raged. The wounded lay dying; many were already dead.

John Hawk, realizing the village was doomed, jumped on Sam and headed out the back road. He glanced back to the village to see soldiers now dragging survivors from the chickees. A Creek shot a child. Ducking the thick vines overhead, John heard a cry like that of a wounded animal. "Help!" And again, "Please help me!"

John Hawk, his hand on his rifle, slid off Sam and held the horse by his reins. He saw that a black woman was in the throes of childbirth. He trusted his horse to carry this woman back to Chumpee, and he lifted her gently onto the horse. Tears of gratitude streamed down her face. He had seldom seen women cry, and the sight unnerved him. "You'll be all right."

He led Sam into the marsh and across a muddy swamp. In the sky, a pair of heron floated free. He waved away a swarm of insects that plagued the poor woman, and ran, with Sam beside him, through the cypress forest. The way seemed longer now that he was on foot than it had with his friends the previous night. Black Dirt and Osuchee were dead.

Chumpee gently helped lift the half-conscious, heavy woman from Sam, and quickly, two older Seminole women came to help with the birthing. Before John Hawk had finished his *sof-ka*, a good stew that Chumpee had made with venison, corn, and wild onion, he heard a wail from the newborn. *A-yah, yah, yah.* John Hawk's heart lifted at the cry. Many thousands of Indians and runaways had died this year in Florida. But here was a new life, a symbol that all was not lost.

The baby, born January 23, 1837, was named for Osuchee, who had died that day, shot in cold blood while carrying a white flag.

22

White settlers and refugees flooding into St. Augustine and Jacksonville wrote letters to the editor. Slaveholders of Florida and Georgia encouraged the war against the Seminoles.

"The war is necessary in order to recapture runaway slaves, Southern property. Seminoles might get the idea that a slave has only to run from the plantation to find freedom," an editorial read.

"The end of the Seminole War would be a sacrifice of national dignity and a clear triumph for the Indians," wrote one "Loyal American."

General Jesup announced the war was won, and he applied for a desk job in Washington. Eight hundred Indians had already arrived at Fort Mellon to emigrate.

General Jesup insisted he would not allow open season in slave hunting in the very fort where the Seminoles were expected to gather to emigrate west. After all the pain of getting the Indians to agree to emigrate, he intended to see that they got off to the West. If slave owners came to Tampa Bay, Jesup would not guarantee them safety.

John Hawk and Luis Pacheco decided to go to Fort Mellon to investigate the conditions of the emigrating Seminoles there. As soon as John and Luis arrived, they were directed to the compound where the blacks were housed. John Hawk did not like the idea of separate compounds for Indians and blacks. That was too dangerous. The very separation confirmed his long-held suspicion that the Seminole War was waged against the runaways, people like himself, rather than against the Indians.

John Hawk, riding Sam away from Fort Mellon, heard hair-raising screams. Peering through a fence, he saw a black man and woman trussed up on the ground like chickens. A fat, red-faced man, beating them with a wooden paddle, would hit the man and then turn and hit the woman as if he were beating carpets. John shouted at him, "Stop! Stop that!"

The fat man put down the paddle, stared at him over the fence, and picked up a rawhide whip. He swung it repeatedly against the helpless victims. The man and woman kept up ear-splitting screams.

A small black boy watching the beating said, "Slave master pay seventy cents for them slaves to be punished that way."

John knelt and asked the boy's name.

"Amos. I help white agent catch darkies for a penny."

In a cold sweat, John Hawk ran and leapt on Sam and galloped back to the hidden hammock in the deep forest. Chumpee met him with "You are returned."

As he ate his roast rabbit, he listened to Osceola and Chumpee discuss General Clinch's plantation, which was now deserted. Clinch, fearful of an Indian raid, had left behind his crops, cows, Spanish horses, and all his furniture. Osceola thought the tribe should move to the plantation, where the children would have milk and vegetables.

Before the day was out, John Hawk moved his followers into the big house that had belonged to General Clinch. Wild Cat's daughter Sparrow, now six years old, lost no time finding a pony and riding it swiftly around the plantation. She rode as well as any boy, and could shoot an arrow straight as any grown Indian man.

For the first time in their lives, Chumpee and John Hawk slept in a real bed in a windowed room. Chumpee shivered with delight at the feel of the clean sheets. She admired the white lace curtains fluttering in the soft breeze. She ran her hand over the handsomely carved four-poster bed of shining mahogany.

She stood in awe before the mirror of the huge armoire.

Indulgently, John Hawk laughed at her, teasing her for being impressed by the white man's trash.

"It is not trash! It is beautiful!" she replied shyly.

In fields of ripe pumpkins, the children played a game, using pumpkins for target practice. When a mother sent a child for a pumpkin, it was a signal for the boy to take a rifle and direct a bullet to cut the stem. The pumpkin rolled with the force of the shot. Sparrow liked this sport and kept after the mothers. "Want a pumpkin?"

But there was little ammunition to spare for games. Luis, who still worked at Fort King, smuggled bullets hidden in his mouth.

General Clinch's blacksmith shop was turned into a school by a former slave who was a skilled smithy. Boys learned to make horseshoes and shoe the animals. Sparrow was the only Indian girl who insisted on learning to shoe the horses.

Even toddlers helped with the chores, some carrying water from the well to dry spots in the fields, some gathering wood or pulling up carrots from the earth.

Luis brought a message from Jesup: "Come to me and we will talk peace."

"So he no longer thinks the war is really over?" John Hawk wondered aloud. "I think we should refuse to talk."

That night Wild Cat arrived at Clinch's plantation. "General Jesup raided a Seminole camp on the Withlacoochee River and captured more than a hundred blacks."

John Hawk said, "We must go bargain with him. If he allows the blacks to emigrate with the Indians, we'll have to agree to leave Florida." Luis conceded.

John Hawk, staring through the French windows at the sun glowing on the orange trees and thick green bowers, saw Sparrow leading Sam to a stump from which she mounted the horse. She rode bareback around the general's grounds, waving and yapping with delight.

John Hawk remembered when Chumpee had gone to her

father's hammock to help Hummingbird deliver Wild Cat's baby. Wild Cat had hoped for a son. When he saw his baby daughter, he had laughed and said, "She looks like a sparrow."

Sparrow was King Philip's only grandchild, and he doted on her. And she had become, as well, the apple of her father's eye.

The air was heavy with the scent of honeysuckle and orange blossoms. In the eaves, doves were *tu-rooing* and flitting to their nests. Birds sang aviary hymns. John Hawk wished he and Chumpee could live here forever.

Framed by the French windows, Sparrow rode around and around on Sam. How that child could ride! John Hawk was impressed by Sparrow, who could already read a newspaper and write a legible letter in English.

"*O-ko-to?*" Chumpee offered John and her brother a bowl of wild onions. While he ate, Wild Cat said Jesup promised that no black or chief would be arrested at the powwow. Wild Cat, never talkative, refused to voice an opinion about whether the chiefs should go to Jesup.

Osceola sat shaking, sweat on his forehead. He had come down with a fever. "I'm sick," he had confessed to John Hawk. "A blackness comes over me and I grow weak." Morning Dew impressed her will on him, insisting he should not go to Jesup.

But John Hawk opted to go with Wild Cat. Sparrow begged to go along with her father, and since he could refuse her nothing, the child sat up on Sam in front of John Hawk all the way to the Fort.

Soldiers met them at the gate and led them to Jesup. Sparrow rode Sam around the Fort yard several times to the amusement of the watching soldiers. The soldiers always tried to treat children and women with kindness. When Sparrow stood up on the trotting Sam, balancing herself with outstretched arms, the soldiers broke into applause. When she tied up the horse and settled on the porch, playing with a corncob doll, several soldiers brought her candy.

Facing Jesup, John Hawk, his heart beating with a strange excitement, wondered if Wild Cat were really as much of a stoic as he seemed. His face was like a mask. Jesup offered only the ends of his fingers for a fishy, distrustful handshake. John Hawk handed the general a white plume and beaded peace pipe from Osceola. For a long moment, Jesup contemplated the gifts. "From Osceola? Maybe these gifts will mean more than an X on a treaty."

Jesup suggested coffee, but John Hawk and Wild Cat said no. Then Jesup said, "Who will be the chief when you reach the West?"

John Hawk recognized the question as a trap. In Jesup's mind there was no question that the Seminoles would go west. But even though Jesup held a hundred blacks as prisoners, John Hawk still hoped to do some bargaining.

"Perhaps Wild Cat should be chief," Jesup suggested, continuing, "Wild Cat's father is King Philip. It's right for you, Wild Cat, to be chief when the Seminoles go west."

"You want us to emigrate," Wild Cat said in a voice that would freeze rivers.

"Where is Osceola?" Jesup asked, for by now, no powwow between the Seminoles and the officers had much value without Osceola's presence.

"He has 'country fever,'" John Hawk replied.

Jesup reached into his pocket and took out his own pipe and a pouch of tobacco. "Take these to Osceola, and tell him I wish him a speedy recovery. Let us meet on the twentieth of October. The path shall be wide and safe from the lodge of Osceola to the Great White Chief's camp."

John Hawk did not trust the fancy speech. He gazed out the window and was startled to see a soldier leading a struggling Indian child on a rope across the compound yard. John Hawk jumped up. An Indian boy being kidnapped? No, it was Sparrow! Like an arrow shot from a bow, John Hawk flew out of the office, leapt from the porch, and dashed to the girl, snatching the rope from the soldier's hand. The soldier stepped back, muttering a warning.

23

In Florida, the season of harvest and the season of growth could be perpetual and parallel. Planting, plowing, and gardening went on year-round. The Seminoles spoke of what it would be like to live in a cold climate where fruit and berries would not grow twelve months a year.

On the twentieth of October, cowbells rang with a hearty optimism as Seminoles approached the meeting ground. Mockingbirds sang. A flock of pink cranes made a streak of color across the blue sky. Wild Cat held aloft a white flag fluttering above him in the breeze. He had decked himself out with a plume of white crane feathers, a silver band around his turban. His red leggings were new.

Convinced now that the Seminoles had to leave Florida, he felt powerless. Nevertheless, he presented a figure of splendor—an Indian chief, proud, colorful, and formidable.

In response to the white flag of the Seminoles, a uniformed soldier signaled with a white flag. John Hawk, Wild Cat, and five other Indian chiefs walked ceremoniously into a circle that had been swept, roofed over, and enclosed by green branches of pine and fir.

Osceola, though he trembled with a high fever, had an electric effect on the soldiers. He had become an American legend, a hero even to his enemies. Now he had malaria and he looked sick. Walking straight, he wore silver ornaments and egret feathers in his freshly washed turban. His hair lay in long braids down his shoulders.

Gravely, soldiers stepped forward and shook hands with each Indian chief. John Hawk's hands were ice cold. The uniformed men seemed eager for peace. Trusting that, John Hawk's heart lifted with hope. These men who had only recently shot at each other now sat in council. John Hawk squatted in the bare circle of ground, the area shaded from the hot sun by the roof of sweet-smelling pine cuttings. Evergreen fragrance mixed with the scent of pipe tobacco. Clusters of coconuts nested under swaying branches of palm trees.

White flags on staffs, stuck into the earth, fluttered next to the American garrison's bright red, white, and blue flag. A warrant officer raised his baton, and the band broke into a rousing march. Even Wild Cat's fierce expression softened slightly; he liked martial music.

After the music, an officer asked the Seminoles to stack their arms. Rising, John Hawk ceremoniously joined the Seminoles in placing his rifle at the designated place outside the circle. He kept his father's ax fastened in his belt. The Seminoles, in full regalia—painted faces, plumes, glittering silver jewelry—had come, hoping for fair negotiations. The officers, wearing clean uniforms and polished buckles, buttons, and brass, had guns at their belts. Since the Indians had relinquished their rifles, John Hawk suggested that the officers set aside their handguns.

Jesup ignored the suggestion and read from an official paper: "Are the Seminoles prepared to deliver up the slaves taken from American citizens?"

Osceola muttered, "John, you talk."

"We did not come to discuss runaways," John Hawk said, gripping his father's ax. "We come to talk peace."

"Why have you not already surrendered the runaways?" Jesup demanded.

"We never surrender runaways," Osceola replied.

Jesup gave a signal. The conference had hardly begun and it was over. White troops closed in on the Indians. With the butt of a rifle, a soldier hit Osceola, who fell to his knees. Suffering chills and very weak, Osceola put up no resistance. He was led off between two armed soldiers. On the verge of collapse, he trembled, his stooped shoulders those of an old man. When a soldier struck Wild Cat with his handgun, the chief lived up to his name, fighting like a tiger, fiercely, knocking out two soldiers before he was subdued. John Hawk, running like a rabbit, hunkered over, zigzagging to avoid bullets that whizzed past him, was soon overtaken by six soldiers. He clutched his ax threateningly but knew he was captured. In the eyes of one of the soldiers, he saw disgust at the cowardly way the Indians had been betrayed. John Hawk had come for a peace powwow, and his indignation at seeing Osceola so humiliated hardened him.

Under armed guard, John Hawk marched behind Osceola, whose hands were bound by a rope behind his back. To the sound of the martial music he loved, Wild Cat marched forward, while Osceola stumbled and forced his weak body to stay upright.

The soldiers led the Indians to the old Spanish fortress of San Marcos, where huge guns pointed in all directions. Approaching the gray walls and lofty battlements, John Hawk viewed the Stars and Stripes flapping in the wind. He felt an ironic bitterness at that symbol of freedom. He remembered the first time he had come to Anastasia Island with Luis. How young and carefree they were then. He recalled Jackson's inauguration as the first governor of the island. He remembered the slave auction. Would he be put up for auction? What would happen to Chumpee and all the families? John Hawk entered the long, dark shadow of the prison fortress.

As the Indians crossed the moat and walked between huge metal doors, chains clanged behind them. Wild Cat and Hadjo with John Hawk found themselves in a small, dark room. John

Hawk discerned only a square of light coming from a small window about eighteen feet above the floor. John leaned wearily against the thick walls of coquina and his fingers felt the broken shell. His spirit was low. He felt his heart breaking.

"Trapped! Like rabbits!" cried Wild Cat, pacing the narrow cell. "Like animals!"

Breathing as if someone had been chasing him, Hadjo stared up at the window and said, "Gotta escape."

John Hawk stared at him. Then upward. "Through that window?"

Hadjo, whose shoulders were broader than the window, said, "You bet."

"That small window?" John Hawk was incredulous.

Wild Cat assured John Hawk they could make it if they could get up there. Wild Cat drove his knife with a powerful thrust into a crevice as high as he could reach. Then, working the knife up to its hilt into the coquina wall, he stood on the shoulders of Hadjo and braced himself to the height of the knife. He stepped up on the knife and just managed to grab the steel bar across the small window. There he clung for a dramatic moment, while John Hawk cheered him. Wild Cat had proven that he could get up to the window. With both hands, he hoisted himself to the hole and tried experimentally to get his head through the space between the bars. He made it as far as his shoulders. Wiggling, he found he could get his shoulders through. "Ready!"

Lowering himself gingerly to his knife, he got a foot on it, then stepped to the waiting arms and shoulders of Hadjo and jumped down to the rescuing embrace of John Hawk. They whispered Seminole words of triumph, excitement running in their veins. "Escape! Escape!" Difficult, but not impossible.

John Hawk remembered the moat outside. "There's a ditch. From that window to the bottom of the ditch is maybe fifty feet. We can't just drop. We'd get killed."

Wild Cat pointed to the forage bags that had been left for

the Indians to sleep on. "Great ropes," he observed.

At the tiny aperture of the heavy door, a deep voice demanded, "What're you up to?"

Quickly, John Hawk hung his coat over the hilt of the knife stuck in the wall. If the guard wanted to know, he could see that John Hawk had improvised a coat hanger.

The guard wanted to know. In a moment, five soldiers were framed in the open doorway. They stared at the coat hanging so high on the wall.

"What's going on?"

There was the chance that the soldiers would confiscate John's ax and Wild Cat's knife.

"Roaches in here," John Hawk explained. "Bedbugs. Lice. I need to keep my coat clean."

The soldiers exploded in a burst of derisive laughter. Hard-faced Hadjo and Wild Cat wore blank expressions. John Hawk tried to be impassive too, but was overcome by his sense of humor and began to chuckle. The guards, pleased with John Hawk, offered him a praline. John, familiar with the sweet candy of melted brown sugar and pecans, broke the candy into three pieces, and he and Hadjo and Wild Cat each had a bite.

The guards, convinced that nothing was amiss, left. Hadjo and Wild Cat lay down on their forage bags. Wild Cat speculated on a moonless night. He knew the track of stars and moon across the celestial heavens and could figure out when there would be no moon. For escape, he said, there must be darkness as deep as the bottomless pit of hell.

❊ **24** ❊

L ying on the floor of the cell, the three captives whispered in Seminole. John Hawk, stone-cold awake, tasted the sweetness of the praline in his mouth and wished for more. But Hadjo have given him sweet hope. Hadjo muttered about something he had been taught by the medicine man. A certain root would shrink a man and help him lose weight fast. They had to get hold of that root.

"Ask the white doctor to get it for us to give Osceola. We will take it for six days. We can make our escape then. In six nights we'll have a moonless sky."

In the morning, Hadjo began crying and moaning when he heard the bolt of the heavy door thrown open. Hadjo clutched his stomach. Wild Cat carried on like a wounded animal. Even John Hawk was concerned about his brothers.

"What's wrong?" demanded the guard. "You were all right last night."

For reply, he got only the bawling and screaming of the three prisoners. John Hawk let loose a screech that could be heard to the top turret of the fortress. He hadn't realized what a good actor he could be! The guard dashed out, leaving the door unbolted. Hadjo nodded toward the door, indicating they make their escape immediately, but John Hawk restrained him.

"We'd be overtaken. No, stick to the plan."

The doctor arrived and examined them. "I can't understand

154

your agony. No fever. No broken bones. No obvious reason for such pain. Was it something you ate?" The doctor's violet eyes watered. He seemed genuinely worried and perplexed.

Hadjo cried, "We got Indian sickness. Like Osceola. Need special herb."

"I looked in on Osceola. He's very sick."

In response to the doctor's request, Hadjo wrote the symbol for the herb on a piece of paper. The doctor said he would try to get it for them, adding, "Osceola has refused all medication. He claims I'm trying to kill him."

John Hawk's eyebrows rode up his forehead. "Why?"

"He learned I'm General Thompson's brother-in-law."

John Hawk forgot to play sick. "You is?"

"I'm a doctor first. I've taken a solemn oath to give the best care I know how to all patients." The doctor's eyes again watered, straining to combat the hostility in the room. The prisoners feared him. They knew about solemn oaths. Yet they had been tricked into coming for a powwow where they were captured.

The doctor urged, "Listen, I'll try to get the herb for you. Please convince Osceola to take it."

John Hawk, hardened by the march under arms to the prison and the betrayal by the whites, had little faith in the doctor. Yet, in a few hours, the doctor returned with the herbs. The Indians, led out to the courtyard, found Osceola there, wrapped in an old blanket. He sat hunched over himself, his face pale, his eyes sunken in their sockets. His hair, so recently raven black, had turned snow-white. John Hawk tried to convince him to attempt an escape with them. "Tell them to put you in the same cell with us. We'll help you."

"You go," Osceola replied. "I have no energy and no heart to try. I was tricked. Captured like an animal. I'm too sick. You go."

John Hawk had never intended to be a killer. He felt in his heart that he was a peaceful person. Yet he was ready to kill anyone who would stop him from escaping.

For the next few days, Hadjo refused the food that was offered the prisoners. They drank the stale water and cider and ate a little of the herb at a time. They felt their bodies shrinking.

The guard repeatedly assured them that a hunger strike would not get them released, but still they refused to eat.

On the fifth night, the guard outside their door began to sing, "No more mistress call for me, no more, no more; no more auction block for me, many thousands gone . . ." His voice, floating into the cell like moonlight, held the last note, deep with sympathy and fellow feeling. Moved, John Hawk wondered if he could make use of this man who sang a slave song in a deep lovely baritone, his voice so different in tone from the black voices John had heard sing this tune.

"Gwine to walk about Zion, I really do believe . . . Gwine to walk about Zion . . ." And here, John could not resist—he joined the singing. Soon Hadjo and Wild Cat, almost as if on cue, sang too, "Sabbath has no end." They sang the chorus with the guard who stood just outside the cell. One white guard, one runaway, and two Indians: "I did view one angel, in one angel stand; mark him down with the foremost, with the harp in his hand. I love God certain . . . I love God sure . . . "

The guard opened the door. "Won't you eat some dinner?"

Hard-faced Hadjo said, "Us sick Indians. Maybe next day we eat."

The guard sat down on the wooden bench, leaving the door slightly ajar. John Hawk thought of the knife stuck in the wall and his ax hidden in the forage bags. They could kill this man or use him as a hostage to get out of the fortress.

"Teach me some Indian songs," the guard requested.

Hadjo said, "Us sick Indians. Maybe next day we teach songs."

The guard could see for himself how shrunken and emaciated they looked, surprisingly so for men who had been imprisoned only five days and had come to the fortress looking robust, vigorous, and bursting with health. The guard worried about Osceola, who seemed determined to die in prison. Osceola had not taken a bite to eat since he was captured.

Hadjo relented. "All right, one war song." He began to sing at the top of his lungs, a message clearly meant for Osceola, informing him through the Seminole words that his friends intended to escape this very night.

Wild Cat joined in, and the guard tried to follow the singing in a throaty voice. John Hawk was impatient with the man's need to socialize. Patience. Patience.

John Hawk's heart was heavy about Osceola. He felt despair as he glanced up at the window. If the escape did not come off, the soldiers might shoot them. Hadjo caught his eye and stopped his song with a sharp word of warning in Seminole. Then Hadjo yawned. Yawning belonged to the white man; Indians never yawned. John Hawk lay down on the forage bag and pretended to be instantly asleep. In a moment, he was breathing evenly, snoring. Wild Cat sat down beside the guard on the bench. He sang an Indian war dance, drumming on his thighs, leaning his head back against the coquina wall. He closed his eyes. "Sick Indians heap weary," he said at the close of the song.

The guard realized the men were weak and tired from fasting. Wild Cat's voice drifted off, and his chest began to rise and fall with the regular breathing of sleep. Only Hadjo remained on his feet, seeming to sleep-walk. The guard gazed from one man to the other and felt himself drowsy, almost hypnotized. He had better get out and lock up. He could hardly afford to be so relaxed with three prisoners, after all. They could have jumped him. He rose, said goodnight, got no reply, and locked and barred the door carefully after him. At the little aperture, he heard the even breathing of the three men.

John Hawk listened to the soldier's departing footsteps. He sat up, clutching his father's ax, and spoke to it. "Help us get out of here." He felt the worn, smooth wood of the handle and drew assurance from its solidity.

Wild Cat said, "Could have tied up that singing idiot, but he might have let loose an outcry."

They laughed softly as they began tearing the forage bags

into strips, John Hawk using the sharp edge of his ax, and Hadjo his knife. Wild Cat braided the strips into strong rope.

In the back of John Hawk's mind, the song repeated itself: "No more auction block for me, no more, no more . . .

With the braided ropes ready, John Hawk, rising, peered through the small aperture to the long corridor where the soldier was expected to be on guard. The sentinel slept. John Hawk heard his snore. He imitated the snore for Wild Cat, who snickered. Their ropes in hand, Wild Cat stood on the interlaced fingers of John Hawk. He plunged his knife back into the crevice of the coquina wall, then pulled himself up on the knife, putting a foot on it. He rose enough to plunge John Hawk's sharp ax into the wood ledge of the small window where the ax held, deeply imbedded.

Wild Cat tossed the knotted strip of the forage bag around the ax head. He fastened the rope and pulled himself up on it, holding on to it with tightly crossed legs. Another forage bag rope he tied around the iron bar of the window. Breathing hard, he forced himself upward—up, up—until he had one knee on the window ledge. He pushed his head out. Wild Cat eased the rope downward from the ax in the ledge. Confident that the rope would reach the bottom of the pit, he began to press himself through the small window. He wiggled out of his loincloth and the shirt he had embellished to wear to the powwow and the beaded belt his wife had made. One by one, he tossed these things out of the window and listened for any sound. Pushing his shoulders first through the window, he almost fell forward as he clutched the rope, twining it around his wrists. He brought his hips and legs after him. The night was unearthly still. Somewhere a cricket sang. In the distance, a dog barked. Nearby, waves smacked the beach.

Oh, for the feel of the sea! He had not bathed for a whole week. Naked, he struggled to lower himself on the ropes, now feet first, the sharp coquina scratching and tearing his skin. The rope held. Downward he slid, his ankles crossed over the rope. He lost a moccasin.

Safely at last in the pit, Wild Cat felt around for his loin-cloth, his embroidered beaded belt, and moccasin. He found his shirt and crawled around on hands and knees until he found his moccasin. He had visions of himself without pants, riding homeward on a stolen horse. At last Wild Cat found the loin cloth. Staring up at the dark opening in the wall from which he had descended, he could hardly see the hanging ropes. He waited impatiently. Where was John Hawk? Why didn't he follow?

John Hawk climbed the ropes up to the window and pushed his head out. He could see the glittering stars. How beautiful the sky was, spread out like his wife's clean hair across the top of the world, black and shining. The night, dark and moonless, as Wild Cat had predicted it would be, was made glorious by the stars shining so brightly. How fine the air smelled. Freedom!

He slid down the rope and almost landed on Wild Cat. He looked up to see the dark shadows of two men doing sentinel duty on the wall. John Hawk and Wild Cat, holding themselves very still, waited now for Hadjo. Hadjo's rope had been fastened through the window in such a way that if the escape were discovered, Hadjo could haul all the ropes back into the cell. If he were in danger, Hadjo was to yank the rope as a signal to John Hawk. Wild Cat and John Hawk were to take off without him. Wild Cat held the end of the signal rope in his hand. Hadjo, the youngest and most agile of the three, was to use the bench in the cell and the ropes to help him get up to the knife and then up to the ax.

John Hawk considered the years he had carried his father's ax. He would never see it again, but it would have helped save his life.

John Hawk and Wild Cat lay flat in the ditch, aware of the dark shadow of rope swinging in the wind. Footsteps. Voices. Two sentinels passed, talking. It seemed ages since John Hawk had slid down the rope. Where was Hadjo? Why was it taking him so long? Far above, he heard scraping sounds at the window and the thick breathing of a struggle. They could make out the head and then the shoulders of Hadjo. From this distance, it looked as if he might be stuck. He might have gotten his head through the window, but the rest of his broad muscular body would not follow through that small opening. Then there was a great grunt. Hadjo came head first, missing the rope altogether and falling fifty feet. John Hawk crawled to his side. He passed his hands over the quiet Hadjo and felt blood.

"I think he's dead!"

Wild Cat felt his pulse. "No," he said in Seminole, "out cold, but alive."

John Hawk and Wild Cat made a stretcher out of the braided forage ropes and lifted Hadjo on it. The action was the work of a few pressured minutes. They carried Hadjo up the side of the ditch and struggled across a field to a stream. Then they set down the stretcher and Wild Cat splashed cold water on Hadjo. Hadjo grunted, "Don't drown me!"

Wild Cat laughed with relief. "You all right?"

"Not really. I'm dead, but my ghost talks."

"Can you stand?"

Hadjo had to be helped up, and John Hawk and Wild Cat supported him as he groaned. "My leg's broke. You go on without me. It's better for you to get away."

"Shut your face," Wild Cat ordered.

The three of them drank from the clear running stream and washed themselves until they felt refreshed. Wild Cat and John Hawk lay Hadjo on the improvised stretcher and carried him between them, the friends running toward the forest. John Hawk knew the streets and led the way.

Dawn broke imperceptibly and faintly paled the soft purple horizon. A mule grazed in the grass, and John Hawk captured it and made a bridle of his sash. He and Wild Cat helped Hadjo mount the mule. In the woods, they found wild oranges and berries. Never had fruit tasted better.

Around noon, they stopped by a clear running creek to

drink their fill of clean water. Naked, the three of them jumped in and bathed all over, rubbing themselves with the sand from the creek bottom. Hadjo washed the dried blood from his leg and examined the bone sticking through the flesh. A medicine man in Hadjo's hammock knew how to set broken bones—if Hadjo made it back alive. At the moment, the pain was so terrible, he didn't care if he lived or died.

Leading the mule along pine-sweet paths, with Hadjo's broken leg supported in a sling John Hawk made of the forage bag strips, they trudged wearily through thick underbrush. They picked dried pumpkins and some green apples. By evening, they rested by a river, where they fashioned fish hooks and dug worms for bait. They fished and built a fire to cook the fish, apples, and pumpkin in the hot coals.

During the night, Hadjo was in great pain. When dawn broke, a clean sky, the color of the inside of a shell, heralded a new day. Wild Cat left John Hawk to help Hadjo dress, and he hunted for food. Without observing his usual caution, Wild Cat stepped out on the dirt road and was face to face with a group of armed, uniformed soldiers.

His heart leapt into his mouth. He ran back into the woods, the soldiers chasing him, shooting bullets all around him. In a thicket, he hid behind a huge fallen tree, holding himself stiff and still. He heard the gunfire bursts still exploding nearby and shouts from the soldiers, and he hoped they would not come upon John Hawk and Hadjo. He waited a long time before coming out, and when he at last got back to John Hawk, he said they had better go on without breakfast.

With Hadjo on the mule's back, they made it at last to Jumper's camp. Here a band of Indians with their families had built rough shelters not far from the Kissimmee River. That night in the red glow of a campfire, Wild Cat told how he had trusted the government officers and had summoned Indian chiefs to the powwow at which they were betrayed. Eight chiefs were still in the fortress. "It was wrong for me to let my concern for my daughter Sparrow lead to the men's capture. We were tricked."

An Indian mother took courage in her mouth to reply, "In the defense of a family, you can do little wrong. You did a father's duty."

A lump formed in John Hawk's throat. That Wild Cat should apologize to the tribe for his behavior upset John Hawk. He was glad when Jumper spoke up: "We know our brother Wild Cat is no traitor. Wild Cat is now the most wanted Seminole in the United States. General Jesup spread the word that if Wild Cat does not surrender, he will kill King Philip."

The campfire spurted. A log fell into the embers and spattered sparks that touched Wild Cat's legs.

"I have no choice. I will not allow my father to die. I cannot have my daughter in danger."

"*Coacoochee*," John Hawk said, using Wild Cat's Indian name for the first time in many moons, "you cannot trust Jesup. He may kill you and Philip both."

A horse galloped into camp, and from the back of the exhausted animal, Luis Pacheco jumped, crying, "Brothers!" Astonished to see John Hawk, Wild Cat, and Hadjo with the chiefs around the campfire, he cried, "General Jesup has ordered that Philip and the other chiefs be put in irons!"

Wild Cat, squatting, buried his head in his hands. "To a chief, that is worse than death. I had hoped to be killed like a brave in battle. But no bullet hit me. I would rather die now in Florida than of old age in the West Country."

Old Micanopy rose heavily and said, "Jesup tells us all Indians must surrender. I promised that the Seminoles with all our runaways will go west. Jesup promises not to separate the runaways from the Indians."

"We have fallen into Jesup's trap before," John Hawk observed. Micanopy's despairing face warned John Hawk that objections had become useless. John remembered the battle in which Micanopy, old, overweight and tired, had jumped into the white man's barricade and started the fight with a knife thrust into Dade. Now Micanopy agreed to give up. He would bring in all the Seminoles, their weapons and their goods, and move to the alien land.

The next morning, leaving Hadjo with the medicine man in Jumper's camp, Wild Cat and John Hawk set off on foot for their own hammock. Chumpee greeted John Hawk with tears in her eyes and bad news.

Osceola was dead.

25

After Wild Cat, Hadjo, and John Hawk escaped, General Jesup had all the remaining Indian prisoners moved to Fort Moultrie on Sullivan's Island. Here a strong brick structure had been built over the old log fort. Burning with fever, Osceola had lay dying there. Morning Dew and her two children were with him when he died.

On the wharf, with crowds of Indian families, Morning Dew recounted to John Hawk how Osceola had breathed his last. He insisted on wearing his turban and three ostrich feathers. "He signed to me. He had no energy to talk. He told me take his bead sash and rifle, and his war belt." Holding her children close to her, she let the tears flow down her face.

Micanopy, his head bowed over his heavy chest, led his people under a flag of truce to the waiting steamer. Behind old Micanopy, the chiefs and a steady stream of Seminoles carried their few blankets and belongings on their backs as they dragged themselves wearily aboard the ship. John Hawk felt his heart breaking.

General Jesup approached him and called his name: "John Hawk!" They did not shake hands, but glared at each other in the warm sun.

Jesup said, "John Hawk, you are chief of chiefs. I know the blacks rule the Indians. I urge you to bring your people to the steamers. You speak English. You must be the principal chief to deal with Washington."

John Hawk replied in a voice like ice, "I am a Seminole and my loyalties lie with the Seminoles." By now, General Jesup had to realize that no arrangement with the Indians would work if it did not also satisfy the runaways. In the crowd, every runaway slave was painted to resemble a Seminole. The blacks were partners of the Seminoles. The blacks had been granted freedom by the Indians and were encouraged to migrate with the tribe to the West Country.

"Here in this sunny land," John Hawk said, "the navel strings of the Seminoles were first cut, and the blood from them sank into the earth and made this country dear to us."

Jesup nodded. "But the condition of your people is now wretched. I ask Washington to give the Seminoles a piece of Florida land — for your own — in return for peace. But the secretary of war told me the policy of Congress is to settle all Indians west of the Mississippi."

Hardly had Jesup left the wharf when Luis arrived with bags of cornmeal. He started up the gangplank to the steamer, dropped the bags, and came running back to John Hawk, crying, "Micanopy and the other Indians have been put in irons aboard the ship."

"In irons!" John Hawk cried aghast. So Jesup had tricked the Indians again.

"They're being sent to prison in St. Augustine."

John Hawk knew what it was to be imprisoned in St. Augustine. He put his wife and Osceola's children on a horse, helped Morning Dew up on another, and he leapt on Sam. They rode back to the camp near Lake Okeechobee, where 400 Indians still lived. In the hammock about half a mile deep into a swamp, surrounded by sawgrass five feet high and deep muddy water, the Seminoles cut through the grass to provide a corridor for their gunfire. They notched the trees to steady their guns.

Wild Cat knew that his father King Philip was aboard ship heading for Fort Gibson in the West Country. Word reached

Chumpee that King Philip was dying. John Hawk's wife mourned her father, sitting on the damp ground, with Morning Dew, both with their long hair unbraided and unkempt. The women wore torn clothes and no shoes, and they wept. They fasted, taking only sips of water now and then.

Wild Cat was hot for revenge. Chumpee no longer begged John Hawk to forget his grievances.

From his vantage point, John Hawk watched the weary uniformed men. Many of the soldiers had only a short time before they were to be mustered out. It was Christmas Eve, 1837, and their hearts had never been in the war. Indians were accustomed to outdoor life in rugged wilderness, swamps, heat, and cold, but the soldiers were not.

The white men did not know how to ride in the jungle. The sawgrass tore their horse's legs. The men's clothing was reduced to rags and their shoes cut to shreds. Some men were down to cutting sandals out of leather harnesses. Many horses had no harness.

John Hawk watched the soldiers, naked from the waist down in the damp cold, as they sewed up rips or patched their pants. John knew that some of the soldiers regarded their greatest challenge finding a dry spot to put down a sleeping bag.

Cudjo rode into the hammock to tell John Hawk that a government ship loaded with rice was wrecked by high waves off the mouth of New River. John Hawk, bored with waiting for a battle and knowing the need for food, took six braves in canoes to New River. His arms felt good as he pushed the paddle through the swiftly running white water. From a distance, he surveyed the situation to make sure the ship was really abandoned and not a trap. He was confident no deaths would be involved in taking the food. The canoes were paddled right up to the edge of the sunken ship. John Hawk went aboard and handed over a huge bag of rice. Then Cudjo and Wild Cat came aboard. The bags of rice were passed from hand to hand and stacked in the canoe.

Back at the hammock, Wild Cat killed a calf, and the tribe enjoyed a rare feast. Warmed by food and drink, John realized this was the anniversary of his father's death. He tried to remember some of the Christmas songs his father had taught him, but only "Oh, Holy Night" came to him, and he hummed it, holding his arm around Chumpee.

Early on Christmas morning, John Hawk could hear the soldiers singing about peace on earth, good will to men. John Hawk had fewer than 400 Indians, but the Seminoles surprised over a thousand soldiers. This Christmas battle would be the bloodiest of the seven-year Seminole War.

Hiding in the timber beyond a stream that wound sluggishly through the swamp, the Seminoles took aim. When a cadre of soldiers wandered into firing range, the Seminoles mowed them down in a fierce blaze of fire. All the men were killed. Another company of soldiers attempted to outflank the Indians. But in the deep marsh, quick movements were impossible and the company lost every officer.

For three hours, the Seminoles kept up a steady barrage of blistering, ear-piercing fire. How long it might have gone on, John Hawk did not know, but at noon, Alligator reached him with a message: Jesup's soldiers had kidnapped Sparrow!

This treachery was what Wild Cat dreaded most, the possibility that his little daughter might be sold into slavery. Immediately, Wild Cat called off the fighting and led the tribe deep into the hammock. The screams of Hummingbird made John Hawk's hair stand on end. So unusual was it to find an Indian woman screaming and out of control that he himself felt disoriented. Hummingbird's eyes rolled in her head, her tongue lolled, her mouth twisted, tears streamed down her cheeks, her hair blew across her face.

"Sparrow!" she screamed. "Sparrow!"

Wild Cat, covered with mud, blood, and gunpowder from the battle, did not take time to change his clothes or eat. He jumped on his tired horse and called for a bundle of sticks. in minutes, hard-faced Hadjo, limping with a whittled cane, and John Hawk counted out one stick for each man of the tribe. Chumpee handed Wild Cat a white flag.

John Hawk on Sam and Wild Cat on a stolen horse galloped to Jesup's fort. Soldiers escorted them to the general's office. Around the Fort, wounded and dying men lay on stretchers, on bed rolls, on porches, or on the bare and damp ground. The agonized moans and screams of the wounded made this Christmas Day one of sadness and despair.

Jesup offered Wild Cat his hand, but Wild Cat refused. He handed the white flag to Jesup. On the flag, Chumpee, months earlier, had stitched clasped hands in a symbol of friendship. Jesup admired the embroidery and, putting the flag on his desk, he sat down and slowly lit his pipe.

Wild Cat, gazing out of the window beyond the general, saw Sparrow run, crying, from a nearby tent and up the porch. She ran into the office, holding out her arms to her father. She was terrified. As he leaned to pick her up, Wild Cat, for the first time in his life, lost control of his emotions and sobbed. He lifted his little girl in his arms, his wet face against hers. Her thin, vulnerable little birdlike bones seemed delicate and as breakable as eggshell. He was shaken for fear of losing her. Pride no longer mattered. Only the life of Sparrow mattered.

Speaking through tears, he said, "General, I've brought you a bundle of sticks. Each stick represents a warrior of my tribe, including runaways. I will bring you for migration a man for each stick."

"Agreed," Jesup said, accepting the sticks.

Wild Cat, holding his daughter, spoke with a trembling voice, "This is our land. Each full moon brings back the spirits of all our warriors who died here. We had hoped to live out our time in peace. Now we must go to the West Country."

Jesup said, "Your feeling for your daughter is a credit to you." What did the man think, that only the whites love their children? "Let us agree," he continued, "that the Seminoles leave after the Feast of the Green Corn."

John Hawk knew that Seminole-white relations had reached their lowest point. "We must try to survive in a land where the sun shines only a few months of the year."

General Jesup offered to shake hands, but Wild Cat refused. He carried Sparrow to his waiting horse. Her hands were fists, and he thought she might have candy, but when he asked her what she had, she replied, "Bullets."

Wild Cat mounted behind Sparrow and urged the horse forward. On the road back to the hidden hammock, John's thoughts were interrupted by the sight of a strange-looking group surrounding a horse-drawn wagon. Intrigued by their colorful dress, silk handkerchiefs wrapped about their heads, beaded embroidered coats and flamboyant lace, John Hawk reined in Sam and asked, "Who are you?"

"Players," replied a raven-haired woman, "actors and actresses."

"What do you play?" John Hawk asked.

"Romeo and Juliet."

"Tell them we want to see a show," Sparrow begged.

"Who are you?" the woman asked, draping a silk scarf around Sparrow's neck and tying it with a bow.

"Seminoles," John Hawk replied.

"Indians!" the actress declared. "I've always wanted to meet Indians."

One of the actors said, "Why do you fight for this land? It's a perfect paradise for mosquitoes, alligators, snakes, frogs, and rats."

"We learned to live in this climate," Wild Cat replied.

"Well, my sympathies are with you in this dirty war."

Wild Cat bowed. "Do your show!"

"Not here," the actress said, with a bright smile.

"Right here, right now!" Wild Cat demanded.

Nervously, the strolling players arranged themselves in a clearing and staged the opening scene of "Romeo and Juliet."

"What strange language," observed Sparrow. She thought she knew English, but the meaning of these English words escaped her. "But I like it!"

John Hawk thought this was likely one of those love stories he had heard when he was a slave on the plantation. The actress stopped speaking, dropped out of character, and said, "Little girl, the play is about two families fighting and the son of one family falls in love with the daughter of the other."

"How does it end?" Wild Cat asked severely.

"Unhappily," the actress shrugged.

"Do the whites like this, that a show ends sad?"

The woman nodded. "Many people love this play."

"Perform the ending," commanded Wild Cat with a fierce gesture. The players conferred about a cue to start the final scene. With the final tragedy dawning on Wild Cat, he stopped them angrily. "Bad ending! The girl must not die!"

He dismounted and approached the young woman playing Juliet. She regarded him with fright. "Give me your scarf and cap!" he demanded.

Reluctantly, she removed the beaded cap from her shining blonde hair. The silk held the warmth of her head. For a moment, Wild Cat resisted the temptation to return it to her. They were whites, and had shown no compassion for his people. Enemies. He went from player to player, demanding tribute, his expression fierce, implacable, taking pearls, jewels, beads, watches, a velvet vest, a wig, and a fancy coat.

He set the little Juliet cap on Sparrow's shining black hair. He burrowed into the theater wagon and turned up a leather satchel. Springing open the lock, he brought up a handful of money.

Wild Cat returned the money to the wagon. John Hawk, amused, tried not to laugh. Wild Cat stuffed his loot into a satchel, tied the bag on his horse, remounted, and they rode off.

Back at the hammock, Wild Cat dressed up in the wigs and costumes of the actors and mimicked their acting, doing a rough version of the play in which he was all the characters.

He had a natural talent for acting, and the Indians applauded, no one more enthusiastically than Sparrow. How wonderful her father was. After such a trying day, he could prance about in beads and wigs.

But John Hawk was heavy-hearted, complicatedly angry. He wanted to do something. Chumpee gazed at him with a steady trust. Damn it. He did not deserve to be trusted. There seemed no alternatives but to leave Florida if he wanted to save the lives of these people. He was now in charge, and he gathered his braves around him. "We must prepare our families to leave for the West Country."

He would miss this lovely land, the oranges growing golden on the trees, the wild lemons and the berries of the woods. The fish caught and carried to the fire. The fresh corn.

"The Great Spirit will guide us," he told his friends. "At night, whenever we camp, we will have our peace pipes and tobacco. We will build a fire under the moon. We will take with us what we care about most—family, friends, dances, songs. When the moon whispers to the dear departed dead, we may listen for the voices of those gone to the Great Spirit. They will give us strong hearts."

The day after Christmas, the sun rose on wildflowers blazing at the edge of the marsh, scarlet and yellow. John Hawk almost resented the beauty of the morning, the air so pure, the water so refreshing.

How he would miss this lovely land!

✳ **26** ✳

Wild Cat kept his promise to Jesup. On the day following the Feast of the Green Corn, the number of warriors who gathered at Tampa Bay to emigrate exactly matched the number of sticks that Wild Cat had given Jesup in return for the safety of Sparrow.

In an orderly march, the Seminoles boarded the ships. Soldiers of the United States Army stood with fixed bayonets. Each Indian was placed under arrest. The chiefs were put in irons, ankles and wrists.

The two hundred Indians were lined up in order of rank, John Hawk first, then Wild Cat, then Jumper, then hard-faced Hadjo, still limping on his broken leg, and the other chiefs. The sub-chiefs, expressionless, followed.

The Indians, in irons, sat down on barrels and rested their chained hands on their knees. Wild Cat forced himself to his feet and spoke in a tense voice: "Coacoochee was a boy here. Now the white man claims the Everglades. I hunted these woods, first with a bow and arrow, later with a rifle. The white man was my enemy.

"We were offered a hand in friendship. We accepted. While taking it, the white man had a snake in the other. His tongue was forked. He lied and stung us. We asked for only a small piece of our land, enough to plant, a spot where we could pray for our dead. Now we go in irons to the West Country."

As a military bugle was blown, the ships slowly sailed from the wharf. An Indian drummer beat a sad song.

The Seminoles, who had hoped never to leave this land, watched the lights of Tampa Bay glittering like morning stars in the soft dusk. The ships moved out on a calm sea. The wooded verdant land receded. Silhouettes of palm trees stood black against the distant sky. The Indians sang a haunting, mournful song that echoed back, back to the sunny water-lapped shores of Florida. The ships plowed across the water in the deepening dusk. Soon no line separated sea from sky.

Glinting in the starlight, the chains clinked on the ankles of the chiefs. The young men sang, hurling their voices at the sky, the world resounding with their songs until the singers, limp, perhaps unable to accept the danger and their plight, felt heart, brain, and soul bursting with grief and longing.

Bibliography

Ballentine, George, ed. *Autobiography of an English Soldier in the United States Army*. New York: 1853.

Bartram, William. *The Travels of William Bertram*. New Haven, CT: Yale University Press, 1958.

Bemrose, John. *Reminiscences of the Second Seminole War*. Gainesville, FL: University of Florida Press, 1966.

Blassingame, Wyatt. *Seminoles of Florida*. Tallahassee, FL: Department of Agriculture, 1959.

Bogges, F.C.M. *A Veteran of Four Wars*. Arcadia, FL: privately printed, 1900.

Buckmaster, Henrietta. *The Seminole Wars*. New York: Collier Books, 1966.

Clay, C.M. *Speech in the House of Representatives of Kentucky*. Frankfort, KY: privately printed, January 1841.

Cubberly, Frederick. *The Dade Massacre*. Washington, DC: Government Printing Office, 1921.

Dunsing, Dee. *War Chant*. New York: Longman's, Green and Co., 1954.

Emerson, William C. *The Seminoles: Dwellers of the Everglades*. New York: Exposition Press, 1954.

Giddings, Josua R. *The Exiles of Florida*. Gainesville, FL: University of Florida Press, 1964.

Hall, Gordon Langley. *Osceola*. New York: Holt, Rinehart and Winston, 1964.

Laumer, Frank. *Massacre*. Gainesville, FL: University of Florida Press, 1968.

Mahon, John K. *History of the Second Seminole War, 1835-1845*. Gainesville, FL: University of Florida Press, 1967.

Motte, Jacob Rhett. *Journey into Wilderness*. Gainesville, FL: University of Florida Press, 1953.

Pratt, Theodore. *Seminole*. Gainesville, FL: University of Florida Press, 1953.

Sprague, John T. *The Origin, Progress and Conclusion of the Florida War*. Gainesville, FL: University of Florida Press, 1964.

Walton, George. *Fearless and Free, the Seminole Indian War, 1835-1842.* Indianapolis/New York: Bobbs-Merrill Co., Inc., 1977.

———. *The Tarnished Shield.* New York: Dodd, Mead and Co., 1973.

Articles

(FHQ: Florida Historical Quarterly)

Moore, John Hammond. "A South Caroline Lawyer Visits St. Augustine, 1837." *FHQ* 42, no. 4 (April 1965), 361.

Moore-Wilson, Minne. "The Seminole Indians of Florida." *FHQ* 7, no. 1 (July 1928), 75.

Porter, Kenneth Wiggins. "The Cowkeeper Dynasty of the Seminole Nation." *FHQ* 30, no. 4 (April 1952), 341.

———. "The Episode of Osceola's Wife, Fact or Fiction." *FHQ* 26, no. 1 (July 1947), 92.

———. "The Founder of the Seminole Nation, Secoffee or Cowkeeper." *FHQ* 28, no. 4 (April 1949), 362.

———. "John Caesar: Seminole Negro Partisan." *Journal of Negro History* 30 (1946), 190.

———. "The Negro Abraham." *FHQ* 25, no. 1 (July 1946), 1.

———. "Negroes and the Seminole War, 1835-1842." *The Journal of Southern History* 30, no. 4 (November 1964), 427.

———. "Osceola and the Negroes." *FHQ* 33, nos. 3 and 4 (January-April 1955), 235.

———. "Seminole Flight from Fort Marion." *FHQ* 22, no. 3 (January 1944), 112.

Reasons, George, and Sam Patrick. "Abraham — Key Seminole War Figure." *Weekender, Washington Star,* January 30, 1971.

Roberts, Albert Hubbard. "The Dade Massacre." *FHQ* 5, no. 3 (January 1927),123.

The author wishes to acknowledge with gratitude personal correspondence and help from Dr. Kenneth Wiggins Porter.

About the Author

BEATRICE LEVIN's first novel, *The Lonely Room* was published in 1950 and she has been writing professionally since, with eleven books and more than four hundred articles and short stories published. She has also published and/or produced five plays.

Beatrice has taught creative writing in Spring Branch school's continuing education for seventeen years, English seminars at Texas Southern University in Houston and a summer course in Shrewsbury, England.

She listed in Contemporary Authors, Foremost Women in Communications, International Biography of Authors and Who's Who of American Women.

If you liked *John Hawk*, you'll like other books in the Council For Indian Education Series. Roberts Rinehart publishes books for all ages, in the subjects of natural and cultural history. For more information about all of our books, please write or call for a catalog.

ROBERTS RINEHART PUBLISHERS
P.O. Box 666
Niwot, Colorado 80544
1-800-352-1985
In Colorado 303-652-2921